Eranox: Cursed

Katlin Murray

Copyright © 2019 Katlin Murray

All rights reserved.

ISBN: 9781690771999

DEDICATION

For friends, and night time adventures.

ACKNOWLEDGMENTS

Thank you to everyone who brought this book to life, from my beta readers to those that assisted with the final edits. This book is what it is because of all of you. As always an extra special thanks to my husband for the cover art, and for always being there for me.

ONE

"You have to tell them you were lost in the woods." Luna's mom pleaded for the fifth time as they got out of the car.

It was a bright cool morning though there was a darkness that hung over Luna as she stepped out of her mom's car.

"Okay Mom, I know." Luna rolled her eyes, they had gone over it at least twenty times before they had even left the house. She knew that the police wouldn't believe her real story anyway, it was too out of this world, and that wasn't an understatement.

"We can't have them looking in the woods, promise?" Luna's mom hissed as she reached for Luna's hand, her voice lowering as they approached the Police Station doors.

"I promise." Luna repeated, squeezing her mom's hand in hers as she reached her other hand towards the brass knob to open the door.

It had only been a day since she had crossed back over from Eranox, the strange world with a portal in the woods behind her house. The Police had already called, insisting that she needed to file her official report so that they could close the case.

She had been declared a missing person, though she had only been gone for a few days, her call to the police on the night that she had gone missing had set off a wild goose chase when they had gone looking for her.

If she hadn't come home they never would have found her, she had been farther away than the woods behind her house. But she couldn't admit that to them, they would only think that she was crazy.

Maybe she was.

The official story, at least the one that she and her mom had agreed to, was that Luna had heard something and called the police and then run to the woods to take the shortcut towards the school to find help, the night had disoriented her and she had become lost, only to return the next night when she finally found the path again.

Lucas still hadn't returned, and she hoped that no one had realized he had gone missing with her. She wasn't sure what had happened to him when she had left him behind, she didn't really want to think about it.

The story they had was clean and simple, and the police weren't likely to question her too much about it, they assumed that she was already embarrassed enough. Everyone in River Falls had probably already heard that she had gotten lost, she was never going to live it down.

"And that was all?" The officer leaned forward, staring into Luna's eyes. She was sure that he must have thought she had come from Bev's party, or had been lurking in the woods looking for something, but that wasn't what she was lying about.

"Yes." She looked down, trying to look embarrassed. It was a shame that she couldn't share the *real* story, about how she had escaped a labyrinth filled with creatures. The real story made her sound much braver than a teenager who had been lost in the forest. But she had to keep it to herself.

"Okay then, you'll need to sign here, and write the date." The officer added, sliding a page and a pen across the table towards Luna.

The officers hid their smirks well while Luna signed her statement, and finally she and her mom were free to forget about the whole ordeal.

They were in and out of the station in less than half an hour, more than enough time to make Luna feel foolish, but enough to give them what they wanted; a closed case.

As Luna walked out of the station doors she felt the weight lifted off of her shoulders, the police wouldn't be prying anymore, but that didn't change much for Luna.

"They must think I'm an idiot…" Luna hissed as the doors to the station closed behind her.

"Sorry it has to be this way." Her mom tried to look serious, but she was hiding a smirk.

Her mother seemed happy, relieved even, that it was finally over and they wouldn't have to deal with the police anymore.

But Luna had questions.

There was so much spinning in her head that she could barely grasp it herself to make sense of it. She had slept since her return, but the nightmares were vivid and woke her in the night, they even managed to slip into her head during the day. She would imagine the dark smoky man walking towards her and jump before she realized that he wasn't really there.

Being alone in the Gateway, surrounded by creatures, it had left her terrified. She wasn't sure she would ever be able to make sense of it, but her mother seemed to know something more. And Luna wasn't going to let it slip away.

"Mom?" Luna asked as they walked down the steps towards her car, "I need to know the truth…"

Her mother's eyes flashed, she looked back over her shoulder, "Not here Luna, wait until we get home." She hissed, moving faster towards the car.

A group of Luna's classmates walked past, staring at her as they made their way towards the school. Luna ducked into the car avoiding them, but that didn't stop their prying eyes from staring. She knew they were whispering, mocking her adventure in the woods with giggles.

Luna wasn't returning to school yet, her mom had agreed to give her a week, and let her story about getting lost in the woods blow over. The way that things worked in River Falls, Luna knew that her classmates would be waiting for her when she returned, and they wouldn't have forgotten about her trip into the woods.

Jessica had already texted her five times, word had already spread and everyone knew about the whole thing, or at least the story they had shared with the police. She knew that when she finally returned to classes she wouldn't hear the end of it, getting lost in the woods for a weekend was a laughable story.

But they could never know the truth.

The truth was, Luna had gone somewhere else, somewhere far away called Eranox, through a rift in the woods behind her house that was guarded by fireflies. But she couldn't tell anyone the truth, only her mom and Lucas knew the real story, and Luna had left Lucas on the other side in Eranox where he belonged.

He hadn't been the friend she had thought he was.

No one seemed to notice that he was still missing, the police hadn't even brought up his name.

Back in the car, Luna's mom was gripping the steering wheel so tightly that her knuckles were turning white.

"Are you okay Mom?" Luna wasn't sure what it was that was bothering her, but she had to know something about that gateway in the woods that she hadn't told Luna yet, and Luna was waiting for her to spill the beans.

"Yeah, I just…" Her mom faltered, turning into the driveway before she could finish her sentence, "I know I owe you an explanation…" She finally admitted, parking the car and turning towards Luna, the pained look in her eyes failing to hide her emotions.

Luna's mom ushered her back towards the house, staring up the street like she expected that there would be someone there watching them.

"Mom, what's going on, how did you know about..."

"Luna not here." Her mom stared down the street, taking Luna by the hand as she rushed towards the door.

Normally they would sit in the living room or the kitchen when they had something to talk about. Instead, Luna's mom led her straight into her office, without even taking her shoes off. She closed the door over and locked it, pulling out a chair for Luna.

"Sit." Luna sat down, staring at her mom while she tried to make sense of it all.

"Mom, what's going on, how did you know about that place?" Luna asked again, from the safety of her mom's office, there were no more excuses for stalling.

Her mom was busy closing the blinds and pulling the curtains across the small window.

She turned, her sad eyes landing on Luna, pleading even.

"Honey, I owe you a real explanation," She sat in her office chair, pulling it towards Luna so she could hold her hand.

"I'm sure I startled you when I saw the ring, I know you have questions." Her mother, spun the ring on Luna's thumb, staring at it for a moment, "Thank you for being so patient with me." She breathed, looking back into Luna's eyes.

"What's going on?" Luna asked again, pulling her hand away, it was as though her mom had become a stranger. Luna had known her for her whole life, through hundreds of moves, and she had never seen this side of her mom before.

Her mom was hiding something from her, Luna was starting to wonder just what kind of person she really was. There was clearly a part of her past that she hadn't told Luna about, what else was she hiding from her?

Her mom leaned back in her chair, staring at the ceiling.

"Eranox," She smiled, "it's where we are from."

"No," Luna stared at her mom, she had finally lost it. Luna remembered seeing her birth announcement in the paper, the fire at the hospital, she knew that her mom was leaving something out.

"Well at least your father and I." Her mom continued, "I know you went to the library, you know you were born here… when there was still a hospital." She shook her head, "But before I tell you about that, you need to know why we came here."

It was all so strange, sitting there and listening to her mother spin a story that sounded more fictitious than real, but Luna had seen the places she was talking about, met the creatures that roamed the Gateway, her brain was hurting from trying to make the connections.

"It was a long time ago Luna, things were once much more pleasant in Eranox." She began slowly, "Though I'm not sure what it has become since we left, your father and I."

"There was a powerful Wizard, one of the High Bloods. He wanted to change things, he wanted to take the universe for himself and create a new world. Eranox stood against him, many others stood against him too. But in his search for power he came to Eranox, and there was a fight. He cursed Eranox and left us. When he did that, the council, the one on our sister world, was forced to seal us off for their own safety."

"Sister world?" Luna laughed.

"We are all a part of one universe Luna, I really should have taught you sooner." She paused, thinking, "Eranox is the birthplace of magic, human magic. It is where the Wizard bloodline was born. There are some who are more powerful than others, certain bloodlines that were harvested to keep the High Wizard bloodline stronger than the others.

"High Wizards?"

"Yes Luna, High Wizards." Her mom sighed, "Your father was the High Wizard of Eranox. You would have been trained to follow him."

"So like royalty?" Luna was confused again, Lucas' father had clearly been the King of Eranox, she didn't think they were related.

"Kings and High Wizards are very different, and much the same." She sighed, "In the our sister world there was a council, tasked with ruling the universe in fairness. Each of the realms had a representative. Your father was Eranox's." She spoke so plainly that Luna could only nod as though it all made sense to her. "There was another Wizard, he didn't like how the council was run, the choices they were making…" She paused.

"And?" Luna was still trying to make sense of it, but she wanted to hear more, it was like a story that she wanted to hear the end of.

"And… he decided that the council was obsolete, that there should be one ruler to reign over the universe."

"Why?" Luna didn't understand much about the other world, but she knew that a council was more likely to make unbiased decisions than one person.

"He felt that too much of it was decided behind closed doors, he had been stripped of his High Wizard status after some indiscretions…" Her mom frowned, "He was upset, and ultimately he blamed the council, so he moved against them." Her eyes looked haunted as she recalled the memory. "He struck Eranox first… so the Wizards wouldn't be able to help…" She whispered.

"What happened to the rest of the council?" Luna asked.

"I don't know." Her mother looked saddened by the thought. "I suppose they survived… if Earth and Eranox are still here, then they must have found a way to stop him."

"So Eranox was sealed off, then how did we get here?" Luna was searching for the fault in her mother's story, the thread of truth that she could cling to.

"There are rifts, Luna, I can't really explain, but the passage in the woods is one of the ways that these two worlds connect. The Gateway connects Eranox to two other worlds, and protects Eranox from intrusion from them. This is one of the worlds it is connected to."

"So the Gateway, was it always there?"

"Yes, the Gateway has been there as long as Eranox itself. The gateway used to be guarded by Knights, it was a means of keeping outsiders from sneaking into Eranox unannounced."

"What kind of outsiders? What other worlds are connected there?" Luna remembered the symbols from the labyrinth, at times there were others that she couldn't place.

"Eranox is connected to Earth and Oro, two of the realms in the Avidauran Universe. The Gateway was built to guard the rifts, and keep Eranox free from unwanted visitors. Not that any ever came from Earth…"

"But the Oreo people, it kept them out of Eranox?"

Her mother laughed. "Yes, it kept the folks from Oro out…if only you knew…" She seemed amused for a moment as though she had stories.

"So Eranox had Knights to guards the Gateway to keep those people out?" Luna wondered.

"Yes. Until the curse was cast."

"And the things in the Gateway? They're from the curse?" Luna asked, trying to picture the maze as a peaceful place, somehow she just couldn't imagine it as anything less than the horror she had seen.

"They were human once." Her mother seemed sad, "I had many friends who served as guards of the Gateway." She explained, "But then the curse turned them, and they weren't the same after."

"They were human?" Luna breathed, remembering the creature that had stalked her in the maze. They looked like things that she couldn't have imagined in her worst nightmares, it was hard to believe that they had once been human, or anything close to. "They didn't look human."

"They were." Her mother nodded, "And then they were turned, they became creatures of immense rage when the sun set. Nothing could pass through the gateway without succumbing to the curse or the cursed."

"Eranox became isolated, there was nothing anyone could do to cure them, so the Kingdom sealed off the Gateway until they could find a way to restore them. They couldn't risk the curse spreading into the other realms, and into Eranox."

"So those *things*..." Luna shuttered, "they've been there for eighteen years?"

"Eighteen years Luna," her mother nodded sadly, "eighteen years of changing, creatures at night, men during the day. Though after all this time I don't know how much of their humanity could be left..."

"And they just locked them up like that?" Luna still wasn't sure that she trusted the Kingdom of Eranox, how could they just leave people in a maze like that, evil or not.

"The curse is contagious, even in their human form they can spread it. Most of them volunteered to stay in the Gateway to keep their families safe. The curse spread though Eranox like a wildfire at first, it took us weeks to contain them and stop the curse from spreading. That was when the King decided that it was time to find help."

"That's when you left?" Luna hadn't realized she was so keen on hearing the story her mother was telling her, she was leaned so far forward in her chair that she nearly fell out waiting for her mom to continue.

"Your father was the last of the High bloodline in Eranox, they chose him so he would escape the curse. I couldn't let him go alone, though I was pregnant with you. I knew that it would be safer for you outside of Eranox until the curse was lifted."

"But he didn't make it." Luna breathed, waiting for her mom to finish.

She nodded, "Your father didn't make it out of the Gateway, one of the creatures bit him. I thought he had died, he spent his last moments, or at least his last moments with me, fighting to keep us safe so we could escape."

"And you just left him there?" Luna pushed herself back into her chair, realizing what her mother had gone through to keep her safe, all the heartache she must have carried all those years thinking that her husband had died to save her.

"I thought he was dead Luna, you have to understand that." Her mother's eyes were watery, Luna had to look away to keep herself from crying. "I had a baby, and a quest…"

"Do you think we can still save him?" Luna asked quietly, though she had never really known her father she could feel the hurt radiating from her mom, the pain of losing him, even all these years later was still there.

"I don't know Luna." Her voice quivered, and still Luna looked away. "When I arrived in this world, I didn't know what to do, it was so different. I lived in the woods for a while until someone took me in. You were born here, and then we began to move. At first I thought that I could still break the curse, but it's been eighteen years Luna, I don't know that we'll ever find a way…"

"So you stopped looking?" Luna stared, her mother's face, still pink from her tears had taken an undertone of guilt.

"The council world is connected to all of the realms, there is a mirror here on Earth that leads to them. I was supposed to find a way to get to them, a way to find help and restore Eranox." She pursed her lips with frustration.

"It was my job to find the mirror, the mirror from Earth to the council in Avidaura. Do you remember all those trips to antique stores, all the mirrors we looked at?"

"Yeah." Luna remembered staring at all the mirrors, and never taking any of them home.

"I was searching for the way back to the council, to find help for Eranox. It was a waste of time…" She trailed off, her eyes watering.

"You didn't find it?" Luna asked, there had been thousands of mirrors, one of them must have been the right one.

"Not even a clue as to where it is. Not even a clue…"

"So you stopped looking." Luna remembered the antique stores, the adventures she and her mother would have trying to find them in the darkest corners of the shadiest back alleys, then one day they had stopped. Luna always thought it was just because she had grown up, her mother had taken a more serious job, and Luna had more school work to deal with.

"I had to Luna, we couldn't keep looking forever. At some point I had to let you live your life. It wasn't fair to you."

"So that thing that I saw." Luna stared at the ring on her finger, remembering the dark man, the one that had scared her into running towards the Gateway in the first place, "That was my dad then?"

"That's his ring Luna, I would recognize it anywhere." Her mom smiled slowly.

"He was here." Luna remembered his shadow standing in the door, a dark void that no light could penetrate.

"He must be trapped in the Gateway with the others." Luna's mom nodded in agreement, she seemed thoughtful for a moment, "That's probably what happened to him…" Her voice grew soft like she though he was trapped with the other creatures.

"No, mom," Luna stared at her mother, trying to get through to her, "he was *here* at the house."

"What?" Her eyes were so wide that Luna could see her own reflection in them. "That's not possible." She stared at the covered window in her office, "Here? At the house? How did he get out of the Gateway?"

"He was here, trying to get in. Like a dark shadow, he looked like he was made of smoke…" Luna shivered, remembering his hand pressed against the glass at the front door. "That's why Lucas and I ran for the woods." Luna answered, her mom stared at her, piecing it together.

"Lucas was with you?" She sighed as though she was relieved that her daughter hadn't gone into the woods alone. Though she made no comment on Lucas' current whereabouts, he hadn't come back with Luna.

"He's not from here." Luna informed her mother.

"He's not?" She sounded surprised, though there was a note of uncertainty. "He's from Eranox…" She trailed off thoughtfully. "He looked so familiar…" She seemed to be wracking her brain for the person she had known that could be a relation to him.

"He is." Luna growled. She was still bitter that she had allowed herself to trust him, that she had followed him like he was a friend, and then he had betrayed her.

"And he stayed there, he didn't come back?" She looked curious, "What happened to him? Was he okay?"

"He's still there." Luna crossed her arms, "He took me to the castle, and they locked me up…" She huffed, "But I escaped, and I came home." She added proudly.

"Escaped?" Her mom seemed confused, "What did you do? Why were you locked up? Were you in the dungeons?" The questions spilled from her mouth as she stared at Luna.

"No…" Luna frowned, "They had me in a room, but I heard them, they weren't going to let me leave."

"Oh Luna," Her mom reached across the gap between them, pulling Luna in for a tight hug, "They would never harm you." She whispered in her ear.

"They locked me up." Luna repeated.

"You are eighteen, Luna, you always had to return." Her mom shook her head, as though Luna wasn't understanding something, "They would never hurt you, you are too important."

"Important?" Luna was utterly confused.

"We were always supposed to return Luna, just not like that."

"I don't understand."

"Isn't that why Lucas came looking for you?" Her mom seemed to understand something that she didn't, "You've reached your eighteenth year." Her eyes flickered, with understanding and a small amount of panic. "They need you to stop the curse." She breathed. "We couldn't find the mirror, and now they want you…"

"Mom, how could I do that, I'm not even from there." Luna nearly laughed, she might have been *from* Eranox, but she hadn't been raised on Earth. How could they expect her to end a curse that her own parents couldn't stop?

"They don't know that Luna." Her mom stood, pacing the room. "They don't know…" She repeated under her breath.

TWO

Luna was still reeling, they had left her mother's office, but the conversation was still repeating itself in her head. She was struggling, trying to piece together what had really happened in Eranox, it still felt like it was just a bad dream.

They had wanted *something* from her, that much she was certain of. But what and why were still escaping her comprehension. Despite her mother's efforts to explain what had happened to Eranox and to her, Luna still couldn't grasp what was at stake. She knew that it meant a lot to her mother, that it was her home world, but to Luna it was just a strange place in the woods, a dark flash in an otherwise normal life.

The day had passed in a blur of tea and toast, the only thing that Luna could stomach while her brain was trying to make sense of it all. Still, her stomach rolled as she tried to sip at her cold tea, sitting on the couch next to her mother, the television glowing softly out of focus across the room.

"So that man I saw, the one who looked like a shadow…" Luna whispered.

"He was your father, I'm sure of it." Her mom answered, biting her lip again.

"How can you know that it was him."

"The ring Luna, he wouldn't have taken it off. He wouldn't have given it to anyone."

"But he gave it to me," Luna still couldn't believe her mother about the shadowed figure. He had chased her from her home and out into the woods, he had followed her and Lucas through the labyrinth. Lucas had said that they needed to get away from him, she had felt the same.

"I know Luna," Her mom was reading her face, "it's hard to believe that he could still be alive."

"I'm not sure that he was." Luna answered, the smoky haze of the dark figure that she remembered so vividly from her nightmares couldn't be more than a ghost.

"He was cursed Luna." Her mom huffed, clearly growing tired of Luna's insistence that the other world didn't make sense.

"What about Lucas then," Luna stared at her mom, "did you know who he was?"

"I didn't, not at first." She admitted slowly, "It became more apparent later, but he hadn't spoken to me yet. I thought you would have a while before they called you back."

"Called me back?"

"Yes, Luna." Her mom sighed for the fiftieth time, "You're a High Wizard's daughter, at eighteen your powers reach their height. They would expect you to help with the curse. I already told you this."

"Why didn't you tell me before?" Luna grew quiet, "About Eranox?"

Her mother paused for a long time, staring at the back door as she chose her words carefully, "I didn't think we were ever going back." She finally whispered.

"What?"

It was the last thing she had expected her mother to say, that she had given up and abandoned her home. She had always seen her mother as a strong person, fighting to keep everything right in a world full of chaos. The number of times they had moved, the number of times her mother had started fresh, just to give Luna a new chance. The words sounded wrong coming out of her mouth.

"You have to understand Luna, I thought your father was dead. I thought there was no hope. We never found the mirror, there is no one that can break that curse. Even you. I didn't tell you about Eranox because I didn't want you to know. You were happy not knowing."

Luna shifted, setting her mug on the coffee table, she wasn't sure how to feel. Her mother was putting her family first, that much could be said, but Luna had seen the Gateway and the creatures. To know that they had been human and just leave them like that was horrible.

"Then why did we move to River Falls?" Luna asked, "Why now, if you've already given up, why come back at all?"

It seemed that her question had struck home, her mother looked uncomfortable at revealing the answer that was coming.

"I didn't know if Eranox was still there, it's been eighteen years Luna." She sighed softly, leaning against the couch, "I knew they would come for you, if they were still there, I just wanted to finish it." She answered.

"Finish it?" Luna didn't understand what he mother was saying.

"They were coming for you Luna." She stared at her mug, "I was going to send them away, this was it, the last stand." She looked into Luna's eyes, pleading with her, "I was going to say no, and then we were going to walk away."

"Were?" Luna caught the hesitance in her voice.

"Your father is alive…"

"And that changes things?"

"It does." Her mom nodded slowly, "It changes everything."

"So you're going to keep looking?" Luna wondered how many mirrors there were that they hadn't seen yet.

"Maybe, I haven't really decided." She sipped at her tea, thoughtfully, "If the curse is still active, then it's too dangerous to return, but there is always the possibility that we find the mirror, get help for them…"

Night had fallen over River Falls and Luna wasn't the slightest bit tired. There were too many thoughts racing through her head, too many questions for her to ask.

"I need to know more." She said simply.

"And you will." Her mother promised, "But for now, I think we should take a break. Tomorrow I can explain more…" Her mom rose from the couch, returning from the kitchen a moment later with an armful of snacks and a pad of paper.

"Why don't you pick a movie, I'm going to make a list of all the things you need to know. I'm sure it's a lot to take in, you've already been through so much." She suggested, handing Luna the remote for the television.

"Okay Mom." Luna shifted down the couch to make room for her mom.

Luna settled in for the evening, biting back all the questions that still lingered on her mind so her mom could write out her list. She was sure there would be questions that her mom wouldn't think to answer, but she could always ask them later.

"Hey mom?" Luna shifted, covering her legs with a blanket, "Do you think if the curse is lifted, we could go visit sometime?"

Her mother smiled, "I'm sure if the curse was lifted we could visit anytime. But you belong here Luna, Eranox is not really your home…"

"But it's your…"

"Not anymore Luna… pick a movie, I've got a lot of questions to answer."

"Okay."

Luna turned back to the television, it felt strange to be doing something so mundane after all that she had been through, after all that she had learned. Knowing that there were other worlds out there made it seem silly to be staring at a television, watching a movie. She set down the remote, trying to act as normal as possible, but she didn't really know what normal was anymore.

Her phone pinged again, Jessica trying to check in on her.

"Who is that?" Her mom asked, watching as Luna checked her phone.

"Just Jessica again." She sighed, setting her phone back down.

"Honey, you should probably call her. She sounds worried…" Her mom gave her a knowing look.

"Fine," Luna agreed, "I'll be right back."

Luna walked down the hall to her mom's office, sitting behind the desk as she pressed the call button.

The phone hadn't even rung when she heard Jessica's voice on the other end.

"Luna? Is that you? Are you okay?" Jessica sounded rushed.

"Hey Jess, it's me."

"Luna, oh gosh, I thought you'd lost your phone or something, you haven't answered me all weekend." Jessica rambled on.

"What's up?" Luna waited for her response, knowing that Jess just wanted to hear her story, as much as anyone else in River Falls did. It was the talk of the town after all.

"How are you? I heard you got lost in the woods?"

"I'm fine," Luna lied, "it was just… a long night." Luna tried to find a way to explain her ordeal to Jess without lying.

"You should have seen the party." Jess went on, "There were police everywhere, looking for you. We even had a search party." Jess gushed.

"Is Bev mad that I ruined her birthday party?" Luna asked, worried that she would suffer the wrath of Bev when she returned to class.

"Oh she's fuming." Jess laughed, "It was amazing…"

"Well I'm glad you had fun."

"Come on Luna," Jess whined, "are you coming back to class soon?"

"I'm taking the week off, trying to let it blow over…" She admitted, wondering if it ever would.

"They'll still be talking about this when they're retired…" Jess admitted, "It's the only exciting thing that's ever happened, "Were you okay though? I heard you were lost?"

"I'm fine." Luna told her again, "Just trying to forget it ever happened."

"What about Lucas?" Jessica whispered, "He wasn't in class today, have you seen him?"

Luna paused, no one had realized that Lucas had been with her. He wasn't exactly missing, he was back in Eranox where he belonged, but chances were Jessica would never see him again.

"He had to go out of town." Luna lied, not sure if that was the best response.

"So you've talked to him? He isn't answering my calls either…" Jessica dug for more information.

"Maybe he changed his number…" Luna suggested.

"Really, so he's not coming back?" She sounded skeptical.

"I don't think he is." Luna answered flatly.

"Are you sure you're okay?" Jessica sounded concerned, "Should I come over, do you want company?"

It was the last think that Luna wanted, trying to act normal in front of Jess would be too hard, "I think I'm just going to watch a movie with my mom and go to bed." Luna answered quickly before Jess could hang up, "But I'll call you tomorrow after school." Luna promised, hopeful that that would be enough time to get her head straight.

"Okay, I'll talk to you tomorrow." Jess sighed through the phone. "Call me if you need anything though, I can be there in five minutes." She promised.

"Thanks Jess."

Luna hung up, she felt sick. Lying to Jessica had been hard, she was a good friend, and had clearly been worried sick.

Luna felt bad that she couldn't share the truth. But knowing Jess, the truth would be too much for her.

Luna stared at her phone for a moment longer, it was new, her mom had replaced her old one that morning before they had gone to the police. It wasn't the same, none of her friends numbers were in it, not even Lucas'. She had thought about him a lot since she had returned.

He had known about Eranox, he had been using the portal in the woods for months without her knowing, spying on her. She had considered him to be a friend, and he had betrayed her.

She would never forgive him.

Luna still couldn't figure out if he had meant to take her into the Gateway that night, or if it had really been a fluke. But that didn't change how he had acted after they had arrived in Eranox. She knew that they weren't going to let her leave, he had let them take her prisoner. He had been a Prince of that strange place in the woods, and hadn't even told her before he had introduced her to the King.

He couldn't be trusted.

Luna heard her mom calling from the living room, she was still staring at the phone in her hand. She tucked it back into her pocket and walked down the hall to the living room.

"Sorry Mom." She tucked herself back in on the couch, the movie had already started, but she wasn't planning on paying much attention anyway.

"Everything okay?" Her mom asked, "Was Jess asking about that night?"

Luna laughed, "Of course she was Mom, it's a small town. Apparently they'll be talking about it until they die…"

"It won't be that bad…" Her mom promised, though there was a note of uncertainty in her voice.

"You're not the one who isn't going to hear the end of it…" Luna mumbled, melting into the couch

"Just don't over think it, okay Luna?" Her mom tousled her hair and turned back to her notebook, "It will all work out." She promised, sounding more sure.

Her mother flipped another page, still scribbling furiously while the movie played in the background.

"How much have I missed out on?" Jessica shifted, trying to stare over her mom's shoulder, she had already written three pages and didn't show any signs of slowing down.

Her mom paused, thinking. "Imagine if you had gone to school but in a different world." She started slowly, "You missed everything that you would have learned there…" She stopped, staring at Luna.

"That much?" Luna gasped, "And you expect to explain it all in a day?" She stared at her mother like she had grown a second head, "That's not possible." She whispered, shaking her head.

"I know Luna, and I'm not expecting you to get it all in a day." She stayed calm, "This," she pointed to the notebook, "is like a cheat sheet." She smiled, "I'll explain as much as I can, but these notes might help you figure some of it out on your own." She smiled.

"Mom," Luna rolled her eyes, "you are insane."

"Sometime I wonder…" Her mom chuckled, turning back to the notebook and flipping another page. "Just watch the movie, try to relax?" She suggested, still writing while she talked.

"I'll try." Luna sighed, turning back to the television.

The movie was already nearing the halfway point, it was a good thing that she had already seen it, otherwise she would be lost. Not that she was really calm enough to watch it anyway, her brain was still spinning, racing at a mile a minute, trying to process everything that had happened over the weekend. She wrapped the blanket around her, letting the warmth sink in. She was finally starting to get tired, all curled up on the couch doing nothing.

Luna's eyes were starting to grow heavy, the scratching of her mother's pen on paper and the quiet sounds from the movie calming her as she started to close her eyes.

There was a flash in the backyard past the tree line, the open curtains on the back door allowed the light to filter into the room for a brief moment as Luna's mom sat upright, startled into action.

"Luna." Her mom edged forward, shaking Luna's leg. "The portal." Her eyes were wide, she was holding back a full blown panic.

Luna jumped up, suddenly wide awake. She stared at her mom for a second, knowing what she needed to do.

"Lock the doors, check the upstairs." Her mom whispered, rushing towards the back door to check the lock and pull the curtain across.

Luna tossed the blanket onto the couch, racing down the hallway towards the front door to check the lock. Her heart was racing like she was back in the Gateway.

That flash from the woods could mean anything. The Knights could be coming after her, or her father might have returned. He had been kind to her in the end, but the form that he took when the sun set still reigned over her nightmares.

She checked the lock and turned towards her mom's office, the curtains were already drawn from their talk earlier, but she checked the window lock before she closed the door anyway.

She knew that her mom would take care of the rest of the downstairs, so Luna hit the stairs two at a time, running up to her room to look out the window.

She was sure that nothing from the other side would be climbing up the side of the house to get in, but she couldn't help herself from edging through her dark room towards the window to look out into the backyard.

She pulled back the curtain, just enough to see into the back yard without being seen by whomever had traveled through the portal.

Though her heart was still racing with worry, she was curious and couldn't help herself.

For a moment she wondered if the portal had just flashed by accident, there was nothing in the yard, nothing moving in the woods. She could barely see the glow from the grove of fireflies, even though the leaves had almost all fallen in the woods. There were no dark shapes moving across the grass, no sign of rustling in the trees. It didn't seem like anything was there at all.

If it was a false alarm she would be relieved, but the terror in her mother's eyes told her that she should be worried that someone or *something* would eventually come through the portal for her.

Why her mother had chosen to buy the house that backed onto the woods was beyond her, there were so many empty properties in River Falls, her mom could have picked any of them. And she had chosen the one house that had a portal in the backyard.

Worse yet, she had known that the portal was there and still chosen the house. Though on some level her mother had always known that they would come for Luna, she had probably picked the house so they wouldn't cause too much chaos in town. A person from Eranox wandering the streets of River Falls was enough to make the front page news for sure.

Luna was about to give up and go downstairs to tell her mom that it had been a false alarm when she finally caught a movement from the corner of her eye.

She waited with bated breath at the window, watching as the shadow moved through the trees, sure that it wasn't a branch caught in a breeze as it moved towards the edge of the woods.

She couldn't tell if it was one person or a group, it could still be the Knights that had followed her. But she knew that there was something there, it wasn't a false alarm.

Luna tugged the curtain closed, her heart racing again, she hadn't realized that for a moment she had been calm; that moment was over.

Without thinking, she dashed back down the stairs, nearly tumbling the whole way down in her hurry to get back to her mom.

"They're coming." She gasped, sliding back into the living room, losing traction with her socks on the hardwood.

Her mom turned, startled by Luna's sudden appearance, her eyes were still wide, she was gripping the couch, trying to drag it towards the back sliding door in an effort to re-enforce it.

"Mom, they're coming." Luna repeated, grabbing the other end of the couch and pulling it towards the door. "I saw them out the window."

"You saw them? How many?" Her mom whispered, her eyes darting to the back door like she wasn't sure that it would hold.

"I don't know," Luna racked her brain, "I just saw the shadow moving through the trees."

"Your father?" Her mom's voice had taken a panicked pitch beyond her normal terror.

"I don't know." Luna hissed, she felt frantic, she didn't know what to do. It was too late to leave and there was nowhere in River Falls that they could go, nowhere that they would be safe. She wasn't going to try for the car again, last time it had failed her.

"To my office." Her mom hissed, reaching for Luna's hand and tugging her up the hall, "We can lock the door." She added, she sounded like she had a plan.

"Mom?" Luna whispered as they closed the office door behind them and her mom locked it.

"Yes Luna?" She ushered her to the other side of the room where they both ducked behind the desk to take cover.

"What if they find us?" Luna whispered, she could hear something outside, moving around the side of the house.

Her mom didn't answer, instead she held her finger to her lips and listened to the sounds outside of the house.

Crunching leaves, the howling sound of wind echoing through the open garage door.

Luna knew she had forgotten something, there was still a way in.

Her heart was racing, it was too late to lock the door to the garage, they were already locked in the office, as safe as they could be given the circumstances. If the intruder found the way in, at least they could still escape through the window.

A shadow passed behind the curtains, Luna and her mother watched, tucking themselves into the desk like it would save them from the shape.

Luna could hear the footsteps walking up the front steps, there was no one else out there, only one person.

That didn't mean the others weren't waiting in the woods, surrounding them, waiting for their attempt to escape.

Luna was panicking, the confined space beside the desk made her feel like she was already trapped, the darkness in the office was like she was back in the Gateway waiting for a creature to pass.

She knew she was panicking, her breaths coming out ragged as she tried to calm herself. Her mother was staring at her, a hand on her shoulder, her eyes calm and serene, trying to ease Luna.

Her breaths started to slow, then there was a knock at the door.

THREE

The knock echoed through the house, Luna found herself holding her breath to stay quiet. She felt her mom growing tense, afraid to move to look at the window, afraid to make a sound.

"Is the front door locked?" Her mom whispered, still staring at Luna, her hands resting on her shoulders.

It did little to comfort Luna, she nodded, "It is, I checked it." She finally answered, staring past her mom at the window.

She didn't know who was out there, but she knew where they had come from, and that was enough to keep her heart racing. Luna stared at the window, waiting for another shadow to cross. She knew it was the Knights, they had come to take her away and lock her up in the castle, "It's them." Luna whispered, tears welling up in her eyes.

Part of her hoped that they would take her mom too, so she wouldn't have to be alone.

"Shh." Her mom leaned forward, pressing her forehead into Luna's and closing her eyes.

The knock sounded again, more impatient this time. Knuckles rapping sharply on the door. The doorbell rang twice to accentuate the sound.

"Hello?" A faint voice sounded from outside, "Is anyone home?"

"It's human." Her mom sighed, leaning back. She sounded relieved. Luna realized that she had feared one of the creatures had escaped the Gateway like her father had.

"It's human." Luna agreed, following her mother's gaze to the office door.

"Should I answer?" She turned back to Luna.

"I don't know, it could be anyone." Luna frowned, "There were Knights following me, they wanted to take me back to the castle… they were in the Gateway, chasing me…"

"Knights don't announce themselves like that." Her mom chuckled, "They would have kicked the doors down if they wanted to get in."

"Really?" Luna wondered if the knocking on the door was just a decoy, there could still be others, waiting for them outside.

The knock came for a third time, followed by another chime of the doorbell.

"Luna? Are you home?" The voice grew louder, "It's Lucas, we need to talk."

"Lucas?" Luna hissed.

She didn't want to talk to him, she was surprised he had come back at all.

"I'm going to have to answer." Her mom stood, walking to the office door.

"Really?" Luna moaned, following her to the hall.

Her mom stepped out of the office and towards the door, pulling back the curtain to check who was standing on the front step.

"It *is* Lucas…" She turned to Luna, "I'm going to let him in, we can't leave him out there." She had already decided.

"Fine." Luna crossed her arms over her chest, waiting behind her mom while she unlatched the door and swung it open.

Lucas was standing on the other side, poised to knock again. He let his arm fall to his side, staring past Luna's mother at her in the hallway.

"Hi, Luna." He mumbled, looking relieved to see her.

"Please, come in." Her mother waved Lucas through the threshold in a strange way, formal and stiff.

Luna stared at her as she tipped her head while Lucas passed.

"Prince Lucas." Her mother bowed deeply, holding the door open for him to enter.

"Thank you for allowing me inside." Lucas stepped into the hall, nodding to Luna in greeting. "You may want to lock the door, in case I was followed." He added quietly.

Luna's mother nodded and closed the door over, quickly checking the locks.

"To what do we owe the pleasure?" She asked, though Luna sensed a trace of hostility in her mother's words.

"You can talk to me normally," Lucas rolled his eyes, "we're on Earth, I'm not a Prince here…" He trailed off, walking towards Luna.

"Are you okay?" He seemed afraid to startle her.

"I've been better." Luna answered, the words coming out sharper than she had expected.

"How did you make it…" He shook his head, "I'm glad you were okay, you shouldn't have gone back in there… not alone like that."

Lucas looked the same as she remembered, though she knew now that he was more. It was hard to think of him as a friend that she had met at school when she knew now that he was from Eranox. He had been traveling through the Gateway regularly, pretending to be her friend to keep an eye on her.

The truth was, she didn't know where they stood. Were they really friends? Or was Lucas a different person, had he merely been pretending all along to get close to her so he could take her away?

Lucas seemed uncomfortable under her gaze, he shuffled his feet, looking down as a thick silence hung in the air.

He smelled of Eranox, Luna hadn't realized that there was a scent, it was earthy and smelled of damp stone and fire. She recalled the Gateway vividly.

"What are you doing here?" She asked, knowing that he wouldn't have traveled through the labyrinth unless he had a good reason, and he appeared to be alone, Luna didn't see any other shadows.

"I needed to know you got out." He answered, still looking down at his feet, "The Knights came back empty handed, and I thought… well you were okay…" He shook his head, "And there was something I need to talk to you about…" He added sheepishly.

Luna stared at him. She couldn't believe him, he had traveled all that way, not to check up on her, but because he had some other motive. She shook her head, her frustration growing by the minute.

"Would you like to come in, have some tea?" Luna's mother cut the silence.

Luna had almost forgotten that her mom was still standing there, she had been so quiet.

"Yeah, sure, that would be nice." Lucas nodded, passing Luna one last pleading look before he followed her mom into the kitchen.

Luna watched as they disappeared around the corner. She checked that her mom had re-locked the front door and peeked out the window. It didn't look like Lucas had been followed, but it didn't hurt to check. You never knew what might happen when you had a portal in your back yard.

By the time Luna followed them into the kitchen her mom had already cleared the table and Lucas was sitting while her mom set the kettle on the stove.

"Are you okay Luna." Her mom whispered, glancing at Lucas with a side stare, "You weren't expecting him, were you?"

"No." Luna answered quietly, following her mom to the table.

Luna sat with her mom across from Lucas. He looked up, and she could sense that he felt guilty about something.

"I'm sorry." Lucas looked down at the table away from Luna, "I don't know why you left, but I am so sorry that you had to go through all of that alone." He glanced up, staring at Luna with pleading eyes. "Why did you leave?" He asked. "I told you the Gateway was dangerous…"

"I didn't leave…" Luna reminded him, "I escaped."

Lucas stared at her a moment longer, the realization filtering through his eyes, "They weren't holding you Luna, you weren't a prisoner. If you had just asked, I would have brought you home. We were going to bring you home…" He sounded sincere.

"Really?" Luna crossed her arms, "The door was locked, I heard them talking…" She shook her head, "They weren't going to let me leave."

"For your own safety, until we figured out what the cursed wanted with you, that *thing* was chasing you, it knew your name…" Lucas turned to Luna's mother.

"Someone was after her." He explained. "I wasn't supposed to take her there, not yet, not before she was ready." He sounded like he was trying to apologize. "But the cursed arrived on your doorstep, I had no choice, there was nowhere else to run. I didn't know she had a stone…" Lucas wasn't making any sense to Luna, but her mother seemed to understand him.

"She didn't have a stone Lucas, not until she came back with the ring." Luna's mother pointed at her daughters hand.

"She had a necklace." Lucas looked at Luna, "Here." He pulled it from his jacket, "You left it at the castle, I was afraid you would be stuck in the Gateway without it."

Luna's mother stared at her, "Where did you get that?" She asked, inching closer to look at the necklace and the red stone dangling from the chain. "That is carnelian… that was the necklace we had when…"

"It's nice," Luna let her mother look at it, "I got it for my birthday." She recalled.

"From who?" Her mother had taken the necklace and was inspecting it quite closely.

"It was hanging on my window with a note." Luna shrugged, she had thought that it had been from Lucas, or her mother even, but they both seemed to wonder where it had come from.

"Do you still have the note?" Her mother asked carefully, sharing a look with Lucas like she had a suspicion.

"I might." Luna turned to leave the room, "Is it really that big a deal?" she asked before she left the room.

"It might be." Her mom called after her.

Luna walked up the stairs slowly, tracing her hand on the banister while she wondered why Lucas was really there. He hadn't gone through the dark maze of beastly creatures just to return her necklace, there was more to it.

If her mother was right, Lucas and the rest of Eranox expected her to break the curse. He wanted her to go back to Eranox, and she wasn't sure that she was ready.

Or that she would *ever* be ready.

Luna found the note in her nightstand drawer, a small scrap of old paper with the simple words *Happy Birthday* written on it.

She returned to the kitchen and handed it to her mom, "Here, that's the note." She sat at the table, waiting for her mother to come to the same conclusion as her; that it was just a necklace, probably a birthday wish from a friend, maybe Jess was the one that had delivered it, Luna had never bothered to ask.

"As I thought." Her mom clutched the paper carefully, then she passed it to Lucas. "It's his handwriting." She sounded sad.

"Are you sure?" Lucas stared at it, but it was clear to Luna that he couldn't tell who her mom was talking about.

"Who's?" Luna asked, "Who's handwriting?"

"Your father's"

"The necklace was from my dad?" Luna stared at her mom, she knew what that meant.

"Which means he had been here before that night that you and Lucas saw him. He has been able to get out of the Gateway the whole time…" Her mom sounded worried.

"That was your dad?" Lucas shook his head, "I had no idea…"

"He was cursed." Luna's mom confirmed. "He didn't make it out with me…"

"He's been there the whole time?" Lucas looked scared, "He isn't here, he didn't find a way… he isn't looking…" Lucas cut himself off like he couldn't find the words.

Luna's mom shook her head.

"That explains a lot…" Lucas stared at Luna again, "That's why she doesn't know about Eranox, or didn't…" He corrected himself.

"Yes." Luna's mom admitted, "We tried, we really did, but I had to protect Luna. She grew up here, Eranox didn't exist to her, I didn't want to ruin it…"

"This changes everything." Lucas seemed at a loss for words. "There is no High Wizard…" He trailed off. "I came back for… but there is no…"

He seemed to be in shock for a moment, Luna couldn't read his face, but she knew that on some level he had thought that her father had been on Earth, that maybe Luna didn't know him because he had abandoned them to continue on the quest to save Eranox.

It had been eighteen years, eighteen years that Eranox had believed that their High Wizard had been out there, trying to save them. To find out that he had been cursed and trapped in the Gateway the entire time, it was a lot to process.

"He can escape the Gateway…" Luna's mom repeated, she looked haunted, "I wonder how many times he has…"

"I don't think it can contain him, he's not like the others." Lucas sounded unsure, but his theory seemed to make some sense to Luna's mother.

"Luna has his ring." Her mother pointed again. "He won't be able to get out without it." She sounded sure.

"He was a High Wizard, there is no telling how the curse affected him…" Lucas answered, draining the hope from the room.

"You're right." Luna's mother whispered. "You're right…"

"He isn't bound like the others, he travels freely in the Gateway." Lucas recalled. "He can speak… "

Luna remembered the dark shadow chasing them through the maze, calling her name, "He was everywhere." Luna agreed.

"That isn't good." Luna's mom stared at the back door, it was still barricaded and covered, she couldn't see the forest beyond. For all they knew he could be traveling through the portal at that moment.

The kettle hissed behind them, filling the room with noise in their silence. Wordlessly Luna's mom got up, returning to the table a moment later with three mugs and a pot of tea. She rested it on the table between them, though no one bothered to reach for it.

Slowly the scent of chamomile tea began to filled the kitchen, Luna could feel it calming her nerves, but the room was still quiet.

The news that her father had been trapped in the Gateway, cursed for eighteen years, it had hit Lucas hard.

He seemed to be working through something in his head. It was clear that he had been hopeful that Luna's father had been on Earth somewhere, he seemed to be struggling to find a way to make something work.

Minutes passed before Lucas finally looked up, a glimmer in his eye indicating that his trip might not be a loss. He leaned across the table.

"What about Luna?" Lucas asked, staring at her mom for an answer, "Is she a High Wizard?" He asked the question carefully as though he were afraid to offend them by insinuating that Luna might not be a pure blood.

Luna's mom turned, staring at her with a questioning look, "She should be, her bloodline is pure." She turned to Lucas, "But there is no way to know, there isn't magic here. She was born in River Falls, she grew up on Earth, there is no way of knowing how that affected her. She was never trained…"

"How can we find out?" Lucas asked.

Luna's mom didn't answer right away, and Luna knew why. The only way they could find out if Luna had High Wizard magic was to send her somewhere with magic, she had to go back to Eranox to get the answer. And her mom didn't want to admit it.

"There is only one way." Her mom answered finally, not giving Lucas the answer.

"I would have to go back to Eranox." Luna whispered.

Lucas seemed to sense that the answer had made Luna's mom uncomfortable, he picked Luna's necklace up off of the table where her mother had discarded it. "You should wear this, at all times." He held it out to her, "It is a High Wizard's stone, a piece of power. You will need it."

Luna took the necklace in her hand, twisting it through her fingers as she stared at it, when she looked up, her mother had tears in her eyes.

"It's time Luna, you *are* a High Wizard, it is in your blood." She reached for Luna's hand, squeezing it tightly. "It's time you wore the carnelian." She smiled, though it was a sad smile. "Your father was gifted that necklace, it was for you when we returned." She pulled out the necklace around her own neck, a small stone of the same color dangled there. Luna had never really noticed it, though he mom had never taken it off.

"Mine was enough to get you here, but once you were born, you would need your own…"

"I don't know why all of this is such a big deal to you two." Luna muttered, unclasping the necklace as she brought it to her neck, "I'll wear it if it makes you happy." She added.

"Never take it off." Her mother advised, "Never."

Lucas shifted in his seat, "There is another reason that I came back…" He admitted quietly.

"I expected as much." Luna's mother stared at him, waiting.

Lucas turned to Luna, the guilt was back, "I just want you to know, it wasn't supposed to happen like that. I had already talked to my father about letting you finish out your school year here. I was going to let your mom know this week that you had more time…" He shook his head.

"You were?" Luna's mom sounded surprised, and relieved even.

"I've been preparing for this for six years." Lucas admitted, "I had to be able to fit in when you returned with Luna." He continued, "Once I got to know her, I realized…" He paused, looking apologetically at Luna, "You didn't know about Eranox." He said slowly.

"And that changed your mind?" Luna's mom sounded surprised.

"It did." Lucas admitted, "She needed time to adjust, and it wasn't fair to just take her."

"You asked for more time?" Her mom sounded relieved.

"I did, and my father agreed. She needed time to adjust before she came back. Before you both came back." Lucas paused.

Luna knew that things had changed, she had already been to Eranox, it was too late to ease into it.

"And then that night…" Lucas recounted as his eyes grew hollow, "I didn't expect you to go through… I was only running towards the school, I forgot. By the time we reached the Gateway, it was too late to turn back, he was right behind us."

Luna still didn't trust Lucas, though her mother seemed to have grown soft.

"I'm sure it all happened so fast..." Luna's mother reached out a hand, placing it on Lucas' shoulder, "But why were they keeping her?" She asked, hesitantly, as though she wasn't sure that Luna's account was true.

"They weren't keeping her, not really." Lucas glanced at Luna, "Yes your door was locked." He admitted, turning away again, "They were afraid you would run, and get yourself hurt."

"Why didn't they tell her?" Luna's mother inquired.

"It had only been one night, and she *did* run...." Lucas sighed, "She's lucky that she made it back at all..." He lost himself in a thought.

The room grew quiet for a moment while Lucas thought. Luna still wasn't sure that he could be trusted, that he had good intentions. But still, her mother seemed to be putting some thought into his words, she seemed to understand what he was talking about.

Perhaps that was the difference, Luna still didn't understand Eranox, she had never seen the curse first hand like the two of them. She had never lived through it, though her nightmares from the Gateway would likely never subside, she hadn't known that they were human while she had been running from them.

"It's getting worse." Lucas finally spoke again, his eyes watered as he stared out across the room. "It's spreading again, and we are running out of time."

"What?" Luna's mother looked haunted, she stared at Lucas for a moment, her eyes slowly moving to Luna, an understanding behind them that Luna never thought she would see.

"The curse made it out of the Gateway..." Lucas stared across the room, "They've quarantined half of the city, but it's not enough."

"It's spreading again." Luna's mom seemed to be remembering something from her past, "It isn't easy to contain." She shook her head.

"Eranox won't survive…" Lucas stared at his feet, "We need a High Wizard." He looked up pleadingly, "We need Luna…"

"No…" Luna shook her head, her voice flat with confusion, "Not me, I don't know anything about curses." She knew that she was right, but Lucas and her mother were both staring at her like she had grown a second head.

"Luna, you *are* a High blood, you are the only one left." Lucas pleaded.

"We knew this was going to happen Luna, we knew it would come to this… just not so soon… I don't know if you are ready for this." Her mother frowned, "We need more tea." She rose from the table to make a fresh pot of tea, though the first pot hadn't been touched at all, it had simply sat on the table growing cold while they talked.

"Luna, I'm begging you…" Lucas whispered as her mother turned away. "There is no other way, trust me, I've tried to think of something…"

"I don't know anything about Eranox." Luna stared at him, frustrated that he was resting the fate of an entire world on her shoulders, "There is no way I can help… we don't even know if I have magic. And even if I do, I don't know how to use it. There has to be another way, my mom is right, I'm not ready…"

"You have to Luna, it's the only way. We really need you." Lucas pleaded.

Her mother returned to the table empty handed, the kettle on the stove slowly warming up again behind her. "What *is* the plan?" She asked Lucas, as though Luna wasn't there at all. "You say you need a High Wizard… but for what?"

"They've found a way." Lucas told her, "But it won't work without a High Wizard."

"They've found a way?" She sounded skeptical, though her eyes twinkled at the possibility. "How?"

"We aren't really sure that it will work." Lucas admitted, "We haven't been able to test it, not without a High Wizard." Lucas shifted uncomfortably, "We need her, she's the only one left."

Lucas stared across the table.

"I need to take Luna back to Eranox."

FOUR

Luna sat quietly at the table, trying to be a fly on the wall while she listened to Lucas as he tried to explain to her mother why he needed Luna to return with him to Eranox.

There seemed to be some sort of plan, though by the sounds of it Lucas hadn't been given very many details on what the plan was, and he was trying to figure it out in his head based on the few scraps of information he *did* have, making it sound like a jumble as he tried to explain himself to Luna's mom.

Though Luna didn't understand much of what was being said, she tried to decipher as much as she could so she could figure it out and save the two of them having to re-explain it to her in Earth terms.

"Sir Hawthorn created a potion, I'm not sure what it contains exactly, some combination of moon wood and saffire or something…" Lucas whispered, "He said that it worked on his testing, separated the curse from the soul, and … Luna… would be able to use it in conjunction with the powers of her bloodline to lift the curse." Lucas leaned forward, avoiding eye contact with Luna.

It was very clear that he had been expecting her father to be the one returning with him, he seemed to shift in his seat uncomfortably every time he had to say her name.

"Using her powers takes practice…" Luna's mom interjected, "She was raised here, where there *is* no magic and she hasn't trained, she won't be able to help."

"I'm not sure that we have any other options…" Lucas shifted again, "Luna … is still more powerful, it is in her blood." Lucas pleaded.

"And how had Sir Hawthorn tested his theory?" She interjected, "Are they even sure that it will work?"

Lucas paused, searching for the right answer to appease Luna's mother.

"He assured the King that it would work, with the aid of… Luna… it could be tested in more detail." Lucas shifted again at the mention of Luna's name.

"Assure?" Luna's mother sighed, "Those are dangerous substances to be mixing… and if I know Sir Hawthorn, and I do, then he hasn't put much thought into what could go wrong. I have seen first-hand what happens when he *tests* new theories…" She sighed again.

"This might be the last shot…" Lucas whispered, his face drawn with sadness.

"And how much is left?" Luna's mom shook her head like she was trying to take back the question. "… How far will it go? How many will the potion work on?" She asked instead.

"I haven't been told." Lucas admitted, "I don't think those answers will be available until it is tested properly…" He added, sounding sheepish.

Though Luna couldn't quite understand the technical matters of their discussion, and a lot of it sounded like garble to her, she was watching her mom's face intently; and she could tell that it wasn't good.

Something in Lucas' plan wasn't sitting right with her mom, and Luna knew that she was about to say no to him, that she was already thinking of a way to keep Luna out of Eranox and harm's way. She could tell that there was danger in the plan that Lucas had presented, though Luna didn't see the harm in trying, her mom clearly knew more about the potions than Luna ever would. All the talk of powers and bloodlines had Luna's head spinning, if all they needed was someone in Luna's family, why wasn't Lucas just asking her mom to go back with him; why did it have to be her?

It had grown late, the kettle was hissing on the stove as the water evaporated from boiling for too long, the sound of the kettles whistle had become a shrill noise in the background giving the conversation more edge than was necessary.

Luna quietly stood up from the table and walked towards the kitchen, letting her mind wander while the conversation continued at the table without her. She had heard all that she could process, they would have to explain it to her in more detail later.

She turned off the stove and moved the kettle over, letting her head clear as the whistling stopped. Luna leaned against the counter while she tried to decipher the conversation that was still happening at the table, though their voices had grown quieter as they debated.

It seemed like Lucas was grasping, he clearly wanted to save Eranox and Luna couldn't fault him for that, she imagined she would feel the same if she knew that Earth was in trouble and she had a way to save it. But there seemed to be very little that he was saying that Luna's mother didn't sigh or roll her eyes at.

She didn't really understand why her mom was giving Lucas such a hard time, he was trying, he really was. And Luna assumed that it wasn't easy, coming back to Earth to beg for help after Luna had already run away from Eranox.

Lucas looked defeated and Luna felt a twinge of guilt. If she hadn't run away, if she had just stayed and let them explain, it would have saved a lot of time. But her mom wouldn't have known where she was, and they would still be looking for her on Earth.

Luna sighed, wondering when her life had become so complicated. She stared back at the table where they were still deep in conversation, there were so many questions that she wanted to ask, but she didn't even know where to start.

The more Lucas tried to convince her mom that his plan would work, the more she scrunched her nose at him. Luna knew that Lucas was running out of ways to explain his plan, but that didn't stop him from trying, and Luna had to admire that.

Finally the table grew quiet, and Luna knew they were waiting for her to return so they could discuss it with her.

She slid back in beside her mom and waited.

"I know all of this doesn't make sense to you." Her mom leaned forward, reaching for Luna's hand.

"We really need you." Lucas finally looked up at her, his eyes pleading, "Would you consider coming with me?" He asked, waiting for her to answer the question that hung in the air.

It was a hard decision, and entire world counting on her to do something that she didn't know how to do, something that was supposed to be in her blood; something that she should have known about her entire life.

Luna stared at her mother, trying to imagine what she must be thinking. She had been raised in Eranox, and there had to be a part of her that wanted to save it.

And then Luna remembered what her mom had told her, she had already given up on Eranox, she had stopped looking for the mirror. Part of Luna wondered if Lucas' plan had sparked something in her, given her a new hope for her home world, but her mother just stared at her.

"You don't have to decide." She whispered, looking into Luna's eyes.

"What?" Luna took her hand back, still staring at her mother. In that moment there was a bitterness in Luna's heart towards her. She had failed to teach Luna anything about Eranox, she had given up on her world. Yes, there had been good intentions, she only wanted a normal life for her daughter.

But Lucas was sitting with them, pleading for help, and she didn't seem to care.

Luna couldn't comprehend how her mother could be so nonchalant about the whole thing.

She considered what Lucas was asking her, the fact that her father had been suffering for eighteen years with the others under a curse was all she could think of, that and the part where her mother had admitted to giving up on them.

"You don't have to go." Her mother repeated, her eyes sad.

"It's the only chance we have." Lucas stared across the table, he looked like he had just been slapped.

"I really don't think she should Lucas." Luna's mother cut in, she had a stern look in her eyes, daring Lucas to defy her. "It's been too long, it's too much to ask of her, it's too dangerous."

"It's the only way." Lucas pleaded.

"Then you will have to find another." Luna's mother had already thought of a response, "Luna isn't trained, she doesn't know enough, there is nothing she can do to help. Bringing her there will only put her in danger, danger that she won't understand. It's too late Lucas, Eranox is already lost…"

"Eranox is still there…" Luna cut her mother off before she could continue making decisions for her, "and my dad is there, suffering. Don't you even care?"

"Luna, you have no idea what he is even asking you to do, you don't know enough to help, you'll only get yourself hurt. It's too late for them." She seemed to have made up her mind about it. For one brief moment, earlier in the day, her mother had changed her mind and considered resuming her quest to save Eranox. Luna didn't know what had changed, something Lucas had said had made her uneasy. Suddenly her mother was prepared to walk away, leave Eranox to perish, and everyone there with it.

"I thought you cared?" Luna was baffled.

"Their plan isn't solid Luna, you'll get hurt. I can't risk it."

"*You* can't risk it?" Luna scoffed, "It's not your choice."

"It's already too late Luna, the curse is spreading again, Eranox will be lost by the end of the week. I know I told you we could help, but it's too late now, there isn't anything we can do anymore… we have to move on."

"What about the people?" Luna shouted, "What about your friends, my dad? What about Lucas?" She rose from the table.

Lucas shifted again, looking quite uncomfortable being stuck in the middle of a spat between Luna and her mother.

"Lucas can stay with us, here." Luna's mother lowered her voice, turning to Lucas who was still trying to make himself look small. "You can stay here, and avoid the curse, we'll make sure you have a good life." She promised, resting her hand on his shoulder.

"Thank you," Lucas nodded politely, "But I can't leave my family, I won't…"

"I understand…" Luna's mother softened again, sitting back at the table deflated, "But Luna can't go with you, she has a life here…"

"I know." Lucas rose, nodding to the table, "If Luna can't come, then I must return. We will have to find another way, I can't sit back and watch the Kingdom die…"

Lucas turned towards the door, taking a deep breath to steady himself before he departed, he was returning to Eranox with more bad news.

"Wait." Luna called after him, reaching for his arm. "I didn't say I wasn't going…"

Lucas looked at her, surprised.

"But I did." Luna's mother cut in, standing again, her eyes glaring at her daughter.

"Just because you gave up doesn't mean I have to." Luna spat, her frustration turning into rage.

She didn't trust Lucas, that much was true, but he wasn't as bad as she had first imagined, and at least he wasn't giving up. Not like her mother, who had clearly decided that she was going to let Eranox implode without lifting a finger to help.

Luna had never met her father, not really, but he had saved her from the Gateway. Without him, she would have been stuck there until Lucas had brought her necklace. Knowing that, she couldn't just leave him in there, she owed him a chance, she had to at least *try* to help him. And if it meant returning to Eranox to test out Lucas' plan, then she was willing to give it a shot.

"I'm going back to Eranox with Lucas." Luna decided. The words escaped her lips in a surprisingly serene way. Her mother stared at her with the same expression as Lucas, disbelief.

FIVE

Lucas sat back down at the table in stunned silence, staring at Luna as she finished making her stand.

The room was silent, even the crickets outside had grown quiet as though they were listening.

"So, you'll come with me?" Lucas asked quietly, "Back to Eranox?" He sounded surprised, "Are you sure?"

Luna sat back at the table, feeling foolish, "Yes." She confirmed, turning to her mother apologetically, "I have to at least *try* to help…" She tried to explain, but couldn't find the words. She had never defied her mother before, she had never had a reason to.

The look on her mom's face was unreadable, and Luna knew that she had hurt her, taking a stand while her mom was only looking out for her best interests. Luna could already feel the guilt welling up in her as she looked away.

"It really would help." Lucas' words came out as a whisper, like he was afraid Luna was still going to change her mind. "It would really help a lot more than you know…"

"I know." Luna nodded, watching Lucas carefully, he seemed more relieved than she had expected.

Her mother hadn't said a word since Luna had made her decision. She sat at the table, staring at Luna, her face frozen and flush with emotions, her eyes watering as she held back tears.

"Are you *really* sure?" Lucas asked again, watching Luna's face for hesitation, "You heard what could happen? You understand that it could be dangerous, that it might not end well?" He lowered his voice, passing a look to Luna's mom, clearly he didn't want to face her wrath again.

Luna considered, she had only been to Eranox once, and it had been terrifying. If the curse was spreading she knew that it would be worse, but she tried to push the fear out of her mind and focus.

"If I don't go with you…" She paused, trying to find the words, "What would happen to Eranox?" She finally asked.

Lucas didn't answer right away, he seemed to be thinking, and that made Luna nervous. She could only imagine what an entire world of creatures like those in the Gateway would be like, she shuttered at the thought.

Lucas finally shook his head, "I don't really know." He answered thoughtfully, "Eranox would probably fall under the curse completely." He added, there was a scared look in his eyes.

"And then there would be no way to save them it would be too late." Luna added, trying to figure it out in her head.

"We've already been forgotten," Lucas agreed, "No one else would come to save us, that would be the end of Eranox."

"And that portal, the one in the back yard… what happens with it?" Luna stared at her mom, "Can they get through, will it come here next?"

Lucas stared at Luna, "I have no idea… I guess it's possible, it would only take one of them…"

Luna nodded her head, she had made up her mind, "Then I have to go with you." She decided again, "I couldn't live with myself if I didn't, if I just let that place disappear… I can't let it come here." She knew that what she had said was true, even then it was hard to forget Eranox. If she just let it go, let it fall under a curse, she would never be able to forget that she had been a coward.

Maybe it would have felt different, if there had been another way to save Lucas' world without going with him, if there had been something else that could be done to stop the curse. But Lucas sounded quite sure that this was it; Eranox's last hope, the last chance they would have to save a world from a horrible fate.

Luna's mother turned, staring at her, "Are you absolutely sure Luna?" She asked quietly, she sounded like she was still holding back tears, "You don't even know what it is they want from you, what they want you to do, the plan… how hard it's going to be." She was grasping for something, looking for any excuse to have Luna stay in River Falls.

There was a hint of fear in her voice as she spoke that Luna couldn't ignore.

"Are you really sure?" She asked again.

"I am." Luna nodded, positive that she wanted to see it through, "It can't be that bad Mom…" She sighed, she wanted to help Eranox, but she couldn't leave with her mom so upset.

"I already lost your father Luna…" She pleaded, "I can't lose you too…"

"I know mom." Luna couldn't find the right words to make it better, she knew that her mom was terrified, "But if I go back… if it works… then you get him back too…"

"I know Luna, that doesn't make it any less dangerous…" Her mom looked away.

"Luna, I want you to be sure." Lucas sighed, "I won't take you back unless you are absolutely certain that you want to, that you can handle it."

Luna felt like she was stuck between a rock and a hard place, she really wanted to go back, she wanted to help, she couldn't live with herself if she didn't; but she couldn't leave knowing that her mother was so worried, she couldn't live with herself if she left her mother like that either.

"Do you think we could have a minute?" Luna asked, "I just need to talk to my mom for a minute."

"Sure." Lucas looked around the house for somewhere to go so they could have some privacy.

"You stay here, we'll go to her office." Luna suggested, saving Lucas the awkward departure.

"That would be easier." Her mom answered, walking with Luna from the kitchen.

"We'll be right back." Luna promised Lucas as she left him behind at the table looking nervous.

There was a thick silence in the air as the office door closed and Luna's mom began pacing beside her desk.

"Mom?" Luna waited for her mom to cool down a little before she interrupted her pacing, she knew better than to bother her while she was deep in thought.

Finally she stopped, turning to face Luna her tears gone, her face set. "I know you want to help Luna, and things *have* changed…" She shook her head, "But if the curse is spreading again…" She trailed off lost in her thoughts as she began to pace again.

"You don't know what it was like there, when it started…" She ran her hand through her hair, her eyes wide with fear, "It's not, it's not safe for *anyone* if the curse is spreading again…" She looked towards Luna, her eyes pleading, there was a terror in them that Luna had never seen before.

Her mother had never talked about her life in Eranox, not once, Luna hadn't even known that it had existed; it hadn't even been a childhood story she had heard about at bedtime. Whatever had happened to her mother there, whatever had happened when she had left Eranox, it had her scared.

"I really think that I should go." Luna sat in the office chair trying to stay calm while her mom continued pacing across the room, "I think I could help, and if I don't go… mom if I don't go, I'm always going to remember that I didn't. Eranox is a *real* place, with *real* people, I can't just let them…" She sighed afraid that she was pushing too hard.

"I know Luna," She shook her head, wringing her hands, "It wasn't easy for me to leave, it still isn't." She sighed, "You don't even know what they want from you, what they *expect* of you… you don't even know how to use your power." She sounded like she had started talking to herself, she didn't glance at Luna once. "You would be helpless, there is nothing that you can do for them… and the danger…"

"Okay mom," Luna waited for her to look back over, "But what if I just go back for a little bit, and hear what they have to say?" She suggested, she didn't want to leave if it was going to be on bad terms with her mom, "If I can't do it, if it's too dangerous… then I'll come home…" She added.

Her mom stopped, staring at her like she was crazy, "And what if they won't let you leave Luna? You are their last hope, do you really think it will be that easy for you? That they will just *let* you go home if you don't feel up to it? Without *you* there is no Eranox… there is nothing without you…"

"We could tell Lucas that it is a condition, if I don't feel right about it then I can come home." Luna crossed her arms.

She knew that she could convince Lucas to go with her plan, and if she couldn't, she had already escaped Eranox once before, "If he doesn't agree, then I don't go." Luna nodded at her mom, sure that it would be enough to make her agree.

"Are you really sure about this?" Her mom finally looked at her, she seemed to have calmed down while she had been pacing, but there was still a hesitance in her words.

"I think I am." Luna answered, she just needed her mom to be okay with it before she made her answer absolute.

Her mom sighed and sat on the edge of her desk, looking far away, "I thought it would be hard to let you leave for college…" She mused, "This is so much harder…"

"Mom…" Luna held back a smile, knowing that she had her mother's blessing to go, "I'm coming back." She promised.

"I know," She smiled sadly, "It's just hard to let you go, especially knowing how dangerous it is. College would have been easier… maybe…"

Luna leaned towards her mom for a hug, "Thank you." She whispered.

"I guess your decision is final." Her mom's voice was muffled in her arm, she squeezed Luna tightly. "Promise you will stay safe, and come home if it's too dangerous." She added, pulling away to give Luna a stern motherly look.

"I promise mom." Luna turned towards the door, "We shouldn't leave Lucas waiting, he's going to want an answer." She added, getting up to open the door.

"I still have questions for him." Her mom followed her back into the hall towards the kitchen.

Lucas was waiting at the table, staring at a cup of tea that he had poured and probably not even touched. He looked up when they walked back into the room.

"Is everything okay?" He asked cautiously.

"Yes." Luna answered quickly, "I'm going with you."

Lucas' eyes lit up, "Really?" He glanced to her mom, knowing that she had some say in the matter.

"There are conditions." Luna's mom slid back into the chair at the table, getting down to it. "If Luna doesn't feel up to it, if it's too dangerous, even if she just changes her mind... you bring her home."

"Absolutely, I will make sure of it." He was looking at Luna's mother as he spoke, promising to return her daughter safely, his face was serious and for a moment Luna felt like she was being exchanged from one handler to another.

"I think I can handle myself." She interjected, before they continued.

"I know Luna, I know." Her mom shook her head, clearly forgetting that her daughter was sitting right beside her. "I just need to know that you'll be safe, that they won't hold you there against your will." She explained, shooting Lucas' another look.

"They won't." He answered before she could even ask.

"What about the curse? It's spreading, will it be safe to travel?" Luna's mother was already moving on to the logistics, not missing a beat as she ensured that everything was in place to keep Luna safe, and bring her home in one piece and un-cursed.

"If we cross just before dawn, the Gateway will be clear during the day to travel." Lucas assured her. "We would arrive at the gates to Eranox while it is still daylight. It would be a full day of travel, but it is the safest way."

"We will need supplies then, and I'm bringing Earth clothes this time." Luna decided.

She had been through the Gateway twice, and each time there had been something that she had wished to have with her. At least this time she could prepare before she had to travel through the winding maze that led to Eranox.

"It's pretty late already." Lucas looked at the clock on the stove, "We should get ready, the Gateway will be closing in a few hours."

"That soon?" Luna's mom stared at her, wiping a tear from her eye.

"We don't have much time to waste, every day counts…" Lucas pleaded, trying not to push it too far, he didn't want Luna or her mom to change their mind.

"Well, if that's the case, then we need to get started." She steeled her shoulders and turned towards the kitchen, "You'll need food." She walked away from the table.

"I'll help Mom." Luna walked to the hall to grab her school bag, it would be the easiest way to carry things. She unzipped the bag and dumped the contents on the floor. With everything else going on she probably wasn't going back to school, ever. Somehow that revelation didn't seem strange to her at all, one trip to Eranox and her whole world had changed, school didn't seem that important anymore.

When she returned to the kitchen her mother was busy filling the counter with nearly everything from the fridge and cupboards. "Oh that will work perfectly." She took the bag from Luna and shooed her away. "Go rest." She insisted.

"Rest?" Luna passed a look to Lucas.

It was already after midnight, there wasn't much time to rest.

"You too, both of you." Luna's mom shooed Lucas away from the table and into the living room. "Get some rest, I'll get everything ready and wake you when it's time to go." She insisted again, tossing a blanket from the couch at Luna.

Luna sighed, her mom had a point; if they were planning on traveling for the whole day they would need to be well rested. Even a small nap would be better than being tired in the Gateway, where you needed to be ready for anything.

"Fine." Luna sighed, stepping towards her mom with her arms out, "Thank you mom." She pulled her in for a hug.

"Get some rest Luna." Her mom whispered into her hair, holding her close, "I want you to be safe out there."

Luna nodded and turned back to the living room.

The couch had been propped against the back door and the comfy chair was still turned to block the hallway.

Lucas had already squished himself into the chair, so Luna made her way to the couch, pulling the blanket over her as she watched her mom work frantically in the kitchen.

It didn't take long for the tiredness to take hold, one minute she was staring at her mom in the kitchen, the next she was being shaken awake, her mom's face in front of her as she opened her eyes groggily.

"Is it time?" Luna mumbled.

Her mom nodded stoically, "Are you sure?" She asked one last time.

Luna nodded.

Her mom moved across the room to wake Lucas from his contorted sleep in the chair.

"Lucas!" Luna shouted across the room while she rolled off of the couch.

He jolted in the chair before her mom had a chance to wake him.

"What?" He sat up, staring at the room while he tried to place himself, "Is it time to go?" He calmed down as he realized where he was.

"Yeah, it's time." Luna answered. "Is the bag ready Mom?" She asked, walking to the kitchen.

Everything seemed to be back to normal, all of the food had been cleared off of the counters and Luna's school bag was sitting on the kitchen table.

"Yes." Her mom answered, "And there are clothes for you there, you should go change." She pointed to a neatly folded outfit next to the bag.

Luna took the clothes and raced up to her room to change. She wasn't sure what her mom had packed, but there wasn't anything from Earth she could think of that she needed to bring, except her necklace that was fastened around her neck. She glanced around her room once hoping that she hadn't forgotten anything too important.

When she returned down the stairs, her mom and Lucas were waiting at the front door. Lucas had the bag on his back and her mom was waving a pair of sneakers at her.

"Wear these, you'll be doing a lot of walking." She handed them to Luna and waited for her to put them on.

A moment later they were walking out into the pre-dawn darkness, around the house and through the back yard towards the woods.

Luna's mom had grown silent, though she had taken Luna's hand in hers and was holding it tightly.

Before they reached the trees, Luna paused. "Mom you should take this." She pried the ring from her thumb and handed it to her mom, "In case you decide to join us, or whatever, you should have it." Luna pressed it into her mom's palm, "I have my necklace now, I don't need it anymore."

"Thank you Luna." Her mom stared at the ring for a silent moment, tears welling up in her eyes as she slid it onto her finger. "Be safe Luna." She whispered, staring into Luna's eyes, her face soft with worry.

"Aren't you coming in?" Luna stared back at the trees, Lucas was waiting on the path a few steps down to give them some privacy.

"I can't Luna," She shook her head, "It's too hard, I can't go back there now…" She pulled Luna in closer for a hug, "Just be safe…" She whispered.

"I will Mom." Luna squeezed her arms around her mom, "I'll come home soon, three days tops." She promised so her mother wouldn't worry.

"Okay." Her mom nodded, letting her go. "I love you."

"I love you too Mom." Luna squeezed her mom one more time before she turned to the trees.

Lucas was waiting for her, he waved at her mom as the two walked farther into the trees, leaving the house behind.

"Is your mom going to be okay?" He whispered.

"I think she is." Luna answered, but she wasn't sure.

She wasn't sure of anything anymore, a day ago she would have thought that she was safe from Eranox forever, the whole world seemed to have turned on its head. She wasn't sure why she had leapt so suddenly at the chance to go back, she didn't even really know what she was getting herself into.

SIX

The grove of fireflies was waiting for them in the clearing. A serene amber glow in the barren autumn forest, beckoning them in as the light bugs flickered in and out of focus in a mesmerizing pattern.

"Are you sure you want to go through with this?" Lucas stopped, turning on the path before they reached the clearing, "This is your last chance to turn back…" He reminded Luna.

Luna had already thought about it enough, though they kept giving her chances to change her mind, "I'm ready." She answered, sounding more sure than she really was.

Lucas nodded, "Okay." He turned back towards the grove, getting on with it. "We'll have about half an hour before the Gateway is clear." He continued, checking the sky overhead through the thinning trees.

"Thirty minutes?" Luna looked up, as though she could figure out how he had made his estimate, the sky was just as dark as it usually was at night, "I think we can handle it, right?" She nodded her head, watching Lucas carefully for his reaction.

She could feel her heart beating in her chest, like she was reaching the top of a roller coaster and was about to take a plunge into the unknown.

Lucas looked like he was feeling the same.

"Yeah, we should be fine." He didn't sound convinced, but he put on a brave face.

"Let's get this over with." Luna suggested, steeling herself for whatever might be on the other side in the Gateway waiting for them.

Lucas paused, "We get through, and we hide until the sun rises." He decided, still not stepping forward, "There is an outcropping near the entrance, we should be able to stay there until it is safe, until the sun rises." He corrected himself.

Luna stopped, "And if it's not?" She asked, reminded of the dangers on the other side of the portal, "And if it is not safe?" She waited for Lucas to answer her, her feet planted firmly on the ground.

If they went through and there were creatures waiting for them, she didn't want to be taken by surprise, she wanted to have a plan; she didn't want to be running for her life.

"Then we run." Lucas looked serious, "And we stay together." He added, sternly.

Luna had been hoping for a different answer, but it seemed that there was only one way to get through the Gateway safely; don't get caught.

"Okay." She agreed, "It's settled then. I think we're good." She nodded, preparing herself for the shift.

Lucas held the bag with their supplies, if they had to run, she was staying with him, no questions asked. She certainly didn't want to find herself alone in the Gateway again, not ever. He also had all of the supplies, and was the only one of the two of them that could navigate back to the doors to Eranox.

He held his hand out to Luna, "Are you ready to go back to Eranox?" He asked, a small smile on his face masking his fear.

Luna put her hand in his, "Ready." She answered.

Hand in hand, they walked towards the grove. Each slow step was another second that they wouldn't have to worry about the creatures in the Gateway. It was starting to seem like Lucas was stalling for time, when suddenly he took a deep breath and ran forward, pulling Luna behind him.

The fireflies were waiting for them, not startled by their quick approach. The tiny flickering bugs swirled in a circle, encompassing Lucas and Luna as they finally approached. The light grew brighter as the two traveled through the rift towards the Gateway on the other side.

It was different than the last time Luna had passed through from the woods behind her house, there was less panic as the light surrounded her. This time she knew what was happening and was able to pay more attention as the transition between the two worlds enveloped her.

The feeling was unreal, like she was being pulled apart and put back together; though surprisingly it wasn't an uncomfortable feeling at all, more like she was being woken up from a deep sleep. She could still feel Lucas' hand in hers, though she knew that if she dared to open her eyes, she wouldn't see him in the light.

And then in a moment it was all over and she could feel the stone beneath her feet and stumbled to stay standing.

They were in the Gateway.

Luna opened her eyes and tensed, trying to take a quick scan of her surroundings to assess the dangers. She could *feel* the change from the woods to the Gateway, her instincts told her that she wasn't safe anymore.

She could hear them, the creatures were calling, growling, their claws clicking on the stone.

They had seen the light, they knew that someone had come through.

Lucas passed her a look, it wasn't good. They could already hear the heavy footsteps coming towards them from somewhere in the depths of the maze. The growls were getting closer. Luna couldn't help herself, she felt frozen to the spot, she knew what was happening, she knew she should move.

The creatures were coming for them.

Lucas grabbed for Luna's hand again, silently pulling her down the path and away from the door that could take her home.

It was officially too late to turn back. The creatures were already arriving, she knew that they had to keep going.

"Move." Lucas hissed, racing around another bend.

Luna swung around the corner behind him trying to keep up. She hadn't been expecting that they would have to run as soon as they had entered the Gateway, she thought that she would have had at least a few minutes so she could catch her bearings before they had to run for their lives. But Lucas wasn't slowing down, and he was dragging Luna along behind him.

Luna glanced back, the eyes were there, watching her, following behind her as Lucas led the way farther into the maze. She hoped that he was going in the right direction to get them to Eranox, it would be a shame if they had to wait until dawn to retrace their steps and start over.

Lucas turned another corner and quickly pulled back a curtain of vines, holding them back so Luna could go inside first. Luna glanced up the path, making sure that it was clear before she agreed to hiding in a hidden dead end. When she knew that the coast was clear she clamored inside, and Lucas followed, carefully draping the vine cover back over the opening so they wouldn't be seen while they waited out the night.

Luna tucked her body against the rocks, trying to make herself small. She could hear the scraping, the howls, the growls. The creatures had arrived at the entrance and were looking for them. Luna wasn't sure how keen their sense of smell was, they weren't too far off, it wouldn't take them long to be found. And if they didn't track scent, her heart was beating loud enough to be heard a mile away. She tried to calm her breathing, only a little longer until the sun appeared, only a little longer and they would be safe for the day.

The half an hour before the sun peaked over the Gateway was the longest of Luna's life. Every moment felt like it lasted an eternity. Each breath sounded like a fog horn calling the creatures closer. She was terrified that they were going to be found.

More than once the shuffling scrapes of a creature passed by them and she was sure that they had been discovered, and yet each time the footsteps had carried on, and they had remained safe.

Until quite suddenly the noises stopped.

Luna waited, the silence somehow scared her even more. It was as though she had lost her hearing, the Gateway had become empty, though it was still dark in their hiding place.

"Is it safe?" Luna whispered after a moment, "Is it dawn?" She wondered where all of the night sounds had gone.

Lucas leaned over carefully, peeking his head out from the vine covering as he checked. "All clear." He pulled back the vines the rest of the way and crawled out, holding out a hand for Luna to follow.

The Gateway was still dark in the early dawn hour, though it was already considerably brighter than when they had first entered.

"Which way?" Luna asked, walking with Lucas to the first path marker.

"Turn here." Lucas didn't even look, it seemed that he had already memorized the Gateway for all of its twists and turns. And when they weren't running from creatures in the dead of night, it was probably easier to travel through.

Luna was more curious than ever, she had decided to return to Eranox, and she wanted to know everything. "Tell me about the Gateway?" She asked Lucas, "My mom told me a bit…" She wasn't sure how much her mom had told her in the grand scheme of things, there were still so many questions. "Like the Oreos, where are they?"

Lucas stared at her like he was holding back a laugh, "The Oreos?"

"Yeah the other world, how does that work?"

"Oh, you mean *Oro*." Lucas chuckled, "Not like the cookie…" He shook his head.

"Oh, well where are they? the *Oro*…" Luna repeated.

"The portal to Oro is on the other side." Lucas pointed over the wall, "If you walked the whole way around Eranox in the Gateway you would find another door. It leads to Oro."

"So the Gateway is to stop them from invading?" Luna used the information her mom had told her.

"Technically, though I haven't seen them, ever." He added, "The Gateway was cursed when I was a newborn." He reminded her, "Though I've heard stories, those Clurichaun were always full of trouble… used to sneak in and play tricks on us. And then the Hobgoblins would come at night and steal things…"

"What is a Clurichaun?" Luna wondered.

"It's a small humanoid creature, they have a strength that is unparalleled." Lucas seemed to be describing them based on what he had heard more than he had seen. "They are only one of the creatures from Oro, that place is quite different from here." He added.

"So are those the three worlds then, Earth, Eranox, and Oro?"

Lucas shook his head, "No, there are nine realms."

"Nine?" Luna stared at him, "And they all come through here?"

Lucas stared at her again, "You really don't know much do you?" He sounded disappointed.

"Only what my mom told me in the last couple of days and what I saw here when we were running." Luna defended herself, she hadn't even known about Eranox a week ago, and Lucas was surprised that she didn't know there were nine realms, it was infuriating.

"Okay, sorry." Lucas softened, "You just seemed to know a bit about Oro, I thought you knew more…"

"Nope."

"Well there are nine realms, but only Earth, Maar and Oro are connected to Eranox." He explained, "think of it like a big circle, each world is connected to the ones beside it by a rift,

Earth is kind of in the middle, they all have a portal there, and then there is the council in Avidaura, they are connected to all the realms by a series of mirrors that they created to unite them all." He paused, "Or at least I heard they used to be…"

"They're the ones that sealed themselves off from Eranox." Luna recalled, "My mom said it was a High Wizard from there that cursed Eranox."

"Yes." Lucas confirmed, "It was."

"Have you ever tried to get to the other worlds?" Luna wondered, "Like Oro?"

"No, I can't get there." He answered.

"It's sealed off?"

"No, I just don't have the right stone." Lucas stared at Luna again.

She knew that she was missing something, something that Lucas thought she should have known, "Well, what is it?"

"You don't have to get so defensive." Lucas sighed, "You'll figure it all out eventually." He looked down, "Earth wasn't easy for me, and I already knew about it…" He admitted.

Luna laughed, "I bet." She chuckled. "So what about stones?"

The rifts are designed to only open for someone with a stone from that realm." Lucas explained, "The Gateway to earth is sealed by Eranox, so you have to have a carnelian." He pointed to her necklace, "But Oro has a different stone."

"What is it?" Luna asked.

"Pyrite." Lucas shook his head, "And you won't find any in Eranox, it comes from Oro. Only the King has one." He paused, "You'd have to steal one from someone who came through, and they haven't bothered us since the curse. Too dangerous for them."

"So your dad has a stone?" Luna was still curious, "Has he ever gone through?"

"I don't know." Lucas answered, he seemed to be getting tired of all of Luna's questions, though she was learning a lot while they walked.

They came to another fork in the road, Luna leaned in to see the markers, though Lucas had already decided which direction they were going.

"Are those markers for the worlds?" Luna asked.

"Yeah, the one that looks like a firefly is Eranox, the circle is earth, and over on the other side there are markers for Oro and Maar, one is kind of squiggly, the other is a bit like a dragonfly. There aren't any markers for Maar, that portal is sealed with magic from both sides." He explained. "The one on the top tells you where the right path leads, the one on the bottom tells you where the left path leads." He continued, pointing to the markers so Luna would understand.

"That's good to know, if I ever get stuck in the Gateway alone, at least I can get out." She added.

"Let's hope that never happens again." Lucas looked stern, "You're lucky you're still alive…"

"What happened to the Knights?" Luna wondered, though she suspected she knew the answer.

Lucas slowed down, "Most of them died." He said slowly, "The horses too…"

"I'm sorry." Luna didn't know what to say, she knew that they had been following her, trying to keep her out of the Gateway. They had died because of her.

"A few returned…" Lucas turned away, "They brought the curse into the city."

"What?" Luna stopped walking, "That's how it started spreading again?"

Lucas shifted uncomfortably, it was clear that he hadn't planned on telling Luna that it was her fault that Eranox was dying. But he had spilled the beans and it was too late to take his words back.

"They had been bitten, and when night fell… they turned." Lucas stared past Luna, not making eye contact. "We locked the castle, and many locked their doors, but by dawn it was too late."

"Where are they now?" Luna wondered, "Are they here, in the Gateway?"

"Some, those that were still sane when the sun rose. But the others took to the woods, and they've come back every night…"

"How long will it take?"

"Eranox will be gone by the end of the week." Lucas answered sharply, "Once they have grown their numbers, mere doors won't hold them back. They will take everyone."

"And then that's it? Eranox is gone?"

"Pretty much."

"What if someone found a way to reverse the curse, after…" Luna was starting to feel the pressure of her quest with Lucas. She was the last High Wizard of Eranox, if she couldn't save them, she wanted to know what would happen.

"No one has ever been turned back." Lucas answered, "They could all be mad for all we know…"

"No one?" Luna was surprised, they had been cursed for eighteen years, and not one of the creatures had ever been turned back. "What about during the day?" She wondered.

"At first they seem normal, the first day at least." Lucas paused, listening around them for a moment. "After that they become…. Unresponsive."

"What does that mean?" Luna asked, following him around another corner in the maze, "They just don't talk?"

"It's like they don't know anyone is there, they are trapped in their body, but unable to move. Most of them just stand there, staring…"

"Isn't there something you can do to help them?" Luna asked, "During the day, when they are human at least."

"They are trying." Lucas turned another corner, "But each passing day they are getting worse. And it's dangerous to keep them in the city."

Luna fell silent, following Lucas as he wove through the winding paths of the Gateway towards Eranox. She knew that it was her fault.

If she hadn't escaped the castle, if they hadn't followed her into the woods and then the Gateway, she didn't know what to think.

She had single handedly caused chaos in Eranox, she had let the curse that they had been protected from for eighteen years pass into the city. She was supposed to be the one to save them, her parents had been sent away to find the cure, and she had ruined it all.

"You seem quiet." Lucas turned another corner.

"Just thinking." Luna still wasn't sure what to say, sorry didn't seem like enough.

"This isn't your fault." Lucas turned another corner, watching her face carefully.

"It really is though." Luna didn't need Lucas trying to make her feel better, "If I hadn't escaped and led all those Knights into the Gateway, the curse would still be contained." It was a fact, and nothing Lucas could say would change her mind. Eranox was in peril because of her.

"The curse was already there Luna, it was there before you were born, you just reminded us that it needs to be stopped." Lucas seemed to have his own opinion, "They've waited for eighteen years, hanging on the hope that your parents were out there finding a cure. Not one of them even tried to stop it themselves." He sounded angry.

"But my parents didn't find a way." Luna reminded him, "Because of me."

"They tried." Lucas reminded her, "To think that Alec has been cursed the whole time… my father… he was counting on him…" Lucas trailed off.

"His name was Alec?" Luna had never heard her father's name before, he wasn't listed in the birth announcement she had seen at the library and her mom had never talked about him.

"Yes, Sir Alec Blackwater, the High Wizard of Eranox."

"What about the other Wizards, the ones from the other council? Where are they from?"

"All Wizards originate in Eranox," Lucas repeated the same thing her mom had told her, "But there is a bloodline in the council realm, Avidaura, that controls the mirror portals. They originated here, but a long time ago."

"So you can't get to them to stop the curse, because they sealed you off…" Luna was starting to understand the severity of it all, "And my parents went to Earth to find the way to Avidaura from there… to get the High Wizards to help?"

"Exactly." Lucas frowned, "But that is clearly not how it worked out."

"How am I supposed to be able to help if Alec couldn't?"

"I'll let the King explain that to you." Lucas turned another bend, "It would just confuse you without an example…" He added.

"Okay." Luna let it slide, she was going to have more questions, but they could wait until she was in Eranox and safe.

"Almost there." Lucas nodded at the path ahead, "Just a few more turns."

"Wow, that was fast." Luna was surprised, the last time she and Lucas had gone through to Eranox it had seemed to take the whole night.

"We weren't exactly taking the regular path that night." Lucas reminded her, "We were kind of busy trying to stay alive…"

"Right." Luna followed Lucas around another bend.

SEVEN

The Gateway had grown slowly brighter as they walked, turning one corner at a time as they wound through the tall stone walls. The daylight rose over the walls as the sun rose higher, washing away all but the most stubborn of shadows as morning became mid-day.

Even Luna felt lighter, knowing that the door to Eranox was only a few hours away had her in high spirits. She wasn't going to be trapped in the Gateway with the creatures of the night this time, she was safe. This time she could *enjoy* the Gateway; not that there was anything really interesting about it.

Moss and vines covered the stone walls in patches, giving the whole place a feel like it had been forgotten. Luna tried to imagine what it had looked like when it was new, before the rocks had started to erode, before the creatures had started to roam the paths, leaving claw marks on the walls. It was like visiting an old settlement, time had taken its toll.

The walls were in desperate need of repair, a few more years and they would come crumbling down, leaving Eranox defenseless against the creatures inside.

"Where do they go during the day?" Luna asked, watching Lucas as he turned another corner, the high walls shadowing the marker that he was using to find his way.

"What?" He slowed down, "Where do they go?" He asked, he hadn't really been paying attention, and Luna's question had clearly caught him off guard.

"Yeah." Luna tried again once she realized Lucas was paying attention, "The *creatures*, where do they go during the day... they have to go *somewhere*..." She added sheepishly, wondering if her question had seemed silly to him.

Lucas turned, glancing down the path behind Luna with wide eyes, his shoulders tensed for a moment and then he looked back to Luna, calming. "They are still here." He answered slowly, "Why, did you see something?" He sounded concerned, and scanned the path again.

Luna felt a chill and glanced over her shoulder to stare down the path they hadn't taken, "They're still here?" She whispered, "Are they dangerous?" She asked, the Gateway didn't feel safe anymore.

Lucas shook his head, "You don't have to worry about them right now." He paused, watching her face to determine what had prompted her to ask the question, "They are... dormant... during the day."

The answer sounded too vague, like he was hiding something, Luna needed to know more.

"What does that mean, *dormant* during the day?" She asked, pressing her hands to her hips.

"Should we take a break?" Lucas suggested, taking the school bag off of his back and setting it to the ground.

"Sure." Luna leaned against the wall beside her, "I could use a water." She leaned forward, not sure if Lucas was guarding the bag or not.

He unzipped it and reached his hand inside, retrieving a water bottle a moment later.

"Thanks," Luna accepted his offer, "but I still want to know what happens to the cursed people during the day..." She trailed off taking a drink from the bottle.

She hadn't realized just how parched she really was. The Gateway was dry and hot, she almost finished the bottle of water in an instant.

Lucas pulled out another bottle of water for himself, "They are still here…" He tried to explain, "But they just… they just stand there." He stumbled to find the words to describe it, "It's like they aren't there at all, it's like they are hollow…."

"So if we see one…" Luna drank the last of her water and leaned over to put the empty bottle back into her bag, "Will it *do* anything?" She asked, looking up at Lucas as he stared out across the path.

"Not really, they are like living statues." Lucas shuttered.

"Have you ever tried talking to one?" Luna stared at him.

"Once, when I was first traveling to your world alone." He nodded, the haunted look on his face startled Luna, "There was no one in there…" He shook his head sadly. "No one…"

Luna nodded, understanding that she should drop the topic. She edged towards Lucas, hoping that they would start walking again so she could put the Gateway behind her. Suddenly the stone maze didn't seem so great in the daytime anymore.

"Just let me know if you see one." Lucas mumbled as he tossed the school bag back over his shoulder and started down the path again, "We can always take another turn… just in case…" He added.

Luna followed him down the path, she felt jumpy and afraid of what they might find in the recesses of the Gateway. There were still so many dark alcoves where the cursed could be hiding.

Luna hurried to catch up to Lucas, walking close to him.

"What happens when they are cured?" She asked in a whisper.

"No one knows." Lucas answered slowly, "You mean, do they turn back to normal?"

"Yeah, will they be back to normal again, or…" She didn't know how to ask, but she wanted to know about her dad. He had been cursed for a long time, her whole life in fact, she had never had a chance to know him. If he was cured, would he be normal after, or would there be lingering effects from the curse?

"I have no idea." Lucas admitted, "I think we will have to find out the hard way, no one has ever been cured before." He tried to smile, falling short at a pained smirk.

Lucas led them down another path, the silence in the Gateway consuming them as they marched forward through the towering walls.

"Turn back." Lucas stopped in his tracks, backing towards the last turn they had taken.

Luna didn't ask why. She stared ahead, wondering what had spooked Lucas as she backed towards the last path.

She couldn't see anything ahead of them, nothing but a dark spot on the wall in the distance. But it had been enough to turn them around, so it had to be something.

Lucas turned them back around and hurried along the path until he found another suitable junction to lead them farther into the Gateway.

Luna stayed quiet until they had walked a few steps into the new path, staring ahead to be sure that there wasn't something else waiting for them before she finally asked, "Was that one of them?"

Lucas looked back over his shoulder, lowering his voice, "I don't know…" He answered, "Something just didn't feel right about that path."

"Okay." Luna agreed, she didn't want to take any chances if they didn't have to. "How much longer?"

Lucas rolled his eyes, holding back a laugh, "Soon, just a little bit farther, the door is up ahead." He pointed to a spot on the path that Luna could see.

"Good." She started walking faster.

Lucas stopped short as they turned the corner and reached the alcove where the door to Eranox proper was hidden. He didn't approach the ornate gate to open it, instead he turned to face Luna with a serious expression on his face that she couldn't read.

"Before we go in, I should probably find out... there is something that I need to know..." He stared at her like he was trying to find the answer to the question that he hadn't bothered asking.

"Well, what is it?" Luna looked behind her, wondering what Lucas needed to know in the Gateway that couldn't wait until they were in Eranox. She half expected to see a cursed Knight standing behind her when she looked back and was relieved to find that the path was still clear.

She didn't really want to stay in the maze any longer than she had to, but Lucas seemed to be stalling. He was still staring at her with that same strange expression on his face, like he was trying to find something.

Lucas lowered his voice, staring into Luna's eyes in a way that made her feel uncomfortable, like he was trying to see *inside* of her.

"Are you a High Wizard?" He finally asked slowly.

Luna stared at him, "What?"

"Are you a *High Wizard*?" He asked again, looking at her like he was trying to figure it out.

Luna looked down at herself, expecting to see a mark on her skin that would tell her, "I don't know." She answered finally, looking back up at Lucas, "You're the one who said I was..." She stared at him like he had gone mad, "Does it really matter if you know right now? Can't we at least leave the Gateway?" She asked, sighing.

She just wanted to get out of there, every moment she was still standing in the Gateway made her feel more uneasy.

Lucas shifted uncomfortably, "Well, I just wanted to know... before we go into the city..." He wasn't telling her something, it seemed very important to him that he have the answer before he opened the doors.

"And now that we are in your world and there is magic, you can test it?" Luna guessed.

"Precisely." Lucas nodded.

"I don't see why it has to be right now, in this place, but alright." Luna crossed her arms, "How do we find out? What is the test?"

He didn't answer right away, Luna was sure that there wasn't a test and he was just trying to figure out how to get his answer by some other means, but he was wasting time. Luna wished that he would just get on with it, the sooner they figured it out, the sooner she could get out of the Gateway, or go home. She really wasn't that picky, she just didn't want to be standing there, in a maze filled with the cursed inhabitants of the city, the sun beating down on her.

She would rather be anywhere else, even math class.

Finally Lucas looked up, there was a twinkle in his eye that told Luna he had finally found his solution, "Let's try something." He suggested. He shrugged the school bag from his shoulders and set it by the door for safe keeping, stepping away from it.

"Hold out your hands like this." Lucas demonstrated, holding his hands out in front of himself with his palms up.

"Alright." Luna humored him, holding her hands out like his, palms up.

"Okay, now focus your energy, imagine it coursing through you. Picture a fire, a fire that will not touch you, but will light the way." Lucas closed his eyes, demonstrating what he was asking her to do. A moment later there was a small flame in his hand, it seemed to spiral out of nowhere, slowly growing to the size of an apple.

"See?" He looked at Luna, "And then put it out." He cupped his hands and the fire vanished. "Now you try."

"Okay." Luna rolled her eyes, she felt silly, standing there holding her hands out while Lucas watched her like she was about to change colors. It all seemed ridiculous. She closed her eyes so she wouldn't have to see Lucas watching her and tried to focus.

She felt warm, she could hear the stone around her crackling.

Luna opened her eyes to fire. It was everywhere, but it didn't seem to touch her. There was a wall of fire between her and Lucas, she could hear him shouting from the other side.

"That's enough Luna! Stop!" Luna clapped her hands together, and the fire went out revealing Lucas on the other side.

His hands were in the air, he had been keeping the flames back. His eyes were wide, and he was staring at Luna like she had grown a second head.

"Well?" She asked, resting her hand on her hip. The answer was clear to her, but she wanted to hear Lucas admit it.

"You're a High Wizard…" He breathed. "Never seen one like it."

"Good." Luna stepped forward, "Now can we get out of the Gateway?"

Lucas shook his head, reaching for the school bag again, "You really have no idea just how powerful you are…" He seemed shocked.

"I made a fire, it was cool." Luna had done what he had asked, she didn't see why they were still waiting in the Gateway. Though she was surprised that she had managed to create something out of thin air, Lucas should have been more accustomed to it, he was from Eranox and he made it seem like it was normal when he had done it. But he was still staring at her like she had two heads.

"I bet if I knew more, like you do, it wouldn't have been so out of control…" She added, worried that he thought she was dangerous, "I won't do it again…" She tried, when he still didn't respond.

"People are going to look at you Luna, they know what you are." Lucas stopped again, "I should probably explain it to you before you meet with the King…" He murmured, more to himself than Luna.

"Explain what, what am i?" He made it sound so ominous.

"You are a Blackwater." Lucas said it like her last name meant something huge. "You are one of the highest bloodlines in Eranox, actually, the highest bloodline in Eranox." He seemed to be racking his brain for a way to explain.

"There were two High Wizard bloodlines, and you descended from Lady Blackwater, she was one of them." He paused, scratching his chin as he tried to explain, "You are more important than the King…"

"No, that's silly. Isn't the King the most important, isn't that kind of the point of having a King?" Luna chuckled, sure that Lucas had explained it wrong.

"The King rules Eranox, but the High Wizard… the High Wizard rules the King…" Lucas stared at her, trying to get his point across, "If you were to marry, your family would take your name, your bloodline is the *most* important in all of Eranox…"

"Really?"

"You are more than royalty Luna. You are a High Wizard. And now that they know… I mean, they *were* expecting your dad, but without him… they know what you are…" He turned to the gates, "Don't be alarmed."

"Alarmed?" Luna asked, watching Lucas' back.

He reached his hand out, touching the brass.

Slowly the door to Eranox began to open, Luna watched as the city came into view.

To her surprise there was a crowd waiting at the door, Knights in their shiniest armor, their heads bowed down in greeting. Luna looked at Lucas, he was staring at her, "They are bowing to you…" He whispered.

Luna stared at him, she had expected a gesture of that kind for their Prince, but not a girl from Earth. Luna tipped her head to them in greeting and followed Lucas forward through the door and out of the Gateway.

"Lady Blackwater." A Knight tipped his head, "Welcome back, your carriage awaits." He waved his hand, leading her through the crowd.

It seemed as though most of Eranox had been waiting at the door, hoping to catch a glimpse of the High Wizard when he returned. Though Luna could tell that they were surprised to see her instead of her father, they bowed to her all the same.

A brass carriage waited on the other side of the gathering, with two brilliant white horses waiting in front of it. Though as Luna stared at them closer, they appeared to have wings and horns. She glanced to Lucas, who seemed to think nothing of it as he opened the carriage door for her.

"Try to look graceful." He whispered as he held his hand for her so she could ascend into the carriage.

Luna took his hand to steady herself, taking the three small steps to the inside. It was plush and red, like something out of a movie about a princess in a far-away story world. Luna sat by the far window waiting for Lucas to join her.

Lucas slid in beside her a moment later and the door closed behind him.

"What's wrong with those horses?" Luna whispered, curious.

"Those are Alicorns, they come from Oro. They are only used for the royal carriage, I know you don't have ones like that on Earth…" He explained quickly under his breath, "You're going to have to smile and wave." He added, pointing to the window, where onlookers were still staring into the carriage window. "They are going to be watching you."

"Oh," Luna plastered a smile on her face and did her best royal wave as the carriage lurched forward on the cobblestone street.

"This is super weird." Luna hissed through her teeth, watching as the heads bowed to her when they passed.

"Get used to it." Lucas whispered back, waving out his own window, "They've been waiting for a High Wizard, it's the only thing that can save them…" He added quietly.

Luna stared out the window at the inhabitants of Eranox, though they bowed to her as she passed, she knew that her family had let them down. Some of them had families out in the Gateway, cursed and lost for eighteen years, others had only recently lost loved ones. They hid their pain well, she could see the hope in their eyes, they were depending on her to save them.

Beyond the wall of onlookers, the rest of Eranox sprawled out. Luna wasn't sure which street they were taking, it looked like the same one that she and Lucas had walked through on her first trip through Eranox, but there was so much about it that was different.

Some of the shops seemed to be boarded up, the gardens were less lush. Though it had only been a day since she had left them, Eranox had already started to fall to ruin.

She wondered what it was like at night, how they kept safe from the curse and where they hid. For the smaller ones it would be all they had ever known, even Lucas didn't remember a world before the curse.

If she *was* able to lift the curse Eranox would change, but how long would it be before it was back to what it was before, before the whole thing had started?

Luna could only imagine that she might get a chance to find out for herself.

EIGHT

When the carriage finally passed through the gates that surrounded the castle and left the city behind the crowd of onlookers disappeared behind them. Luna slumped forward in her seat, her face aching from all of the smiling and waving.

There were more people in Eranox than she had imagined, certainly more than she had seen during her last short visit. They seemed to have come from nowhere, filling the streets, watching from windows, standing on rooftops. And they had all stared at her the same, they had been expecting someone else, but she would have to do.

"Are you alright over there?" Lucas laughed.

"My face hurts." Luna pressed her hands against her cheeks, trying to get the feeling back in her chin.

"You'll get used to it." Lucas smiled, handing over her school bag as he watched her face with a smirk.

"Is it always going to be like that?" She wondered, remembering her first arrival in Eranox and how the inhabitants had stared at Lucas, back then she was practically invisible.

"For now at least," Lucas looked out the window as the castle approached, "It has been a long time since we have had a High Wizard, some of them have never even seen one until now. I'm not sure they know how to act around you to be honest... it's been so long, even *I* don't know how..." He shrugged his shoulders turning back into the carriage, "You give them hope." He added, leaning forward to reach for the door. "You have your bag, I'll let you take your things from here." He smiled as the carriage finally jolted to a stop.

Luna looped the strap of her bag over her shoulder and glanced out the window, they had arrived at the doors to the castle and another crowd was waiting.

"Remember that you can ask for me if you need anything." Lucas added, his hand hovering over the handle.

"Wait, you're not coming with me?" Luna asked, surprised, "Where are you going?" She had thought Lucas would be with her for the whole trip to Eranox, to help guide her through it. She wasn't sure that she would be okay on her own to navigate his strange world, especially if she needed to use those powers again; she had no idea how to control them. "How am I supposed to act?" Her eyes were wide, "What are High Wizards normally like?"

"Just act like you are supposed to be the one who is here, *be* Lady Blackwater, you will be fine." Lucas assured her.

"And what about you, where will you be?"

Lucas shook his head disappointedly as though it was not his decision to make, "I'll be around, but they need *you* not me…" He trailed off sheepishly.

The door opened before Luna could say anything else and Lucas climbed out of the carriage, waiting at the bottom of the steps to help Luna down.

She held her bag over one shoulder and stepped outside, not sure what to expect.

A line of men with trumpets and silly hats stood on the front steps, playing some strange melody to greet them as they walked from the carriage towards the front steps of the castle. Luna felt her face flush, she was sure that all of the extra show was meant for the other High Wizard they had been expecting, not for her.

"Lady Blackwater," Margie curtsied, standing at the head of a line of servants waiting to greet them, "I am so glad that you are safe." Her face flushed as she looked down guiltily.

Luna tipped her head in greeting, not sure what to say. It hadn't been Margie's fault that Luna had escaped her room and traveled home through the Gateway in the dead of night, not really. She could tell that she had caused the kind servant some grief with her unusual disappearance.

"They are going to take you back to your room." Lucas whispered, letting go of her hand slowly, "I will see you very soon, I promise." He added, stepping away to let Luna go.

Luna nodded and walked towards Margie nervously, it was nice to see a familiar face. At least she knew that she wouldn't be alone.

"This way, Lady Blackwater." Margie smiled, leading Luna into the castle through the towering ornate doors that waited open for them.

Luna followed Margie through the great doors into the castle, leaving Lucas and the greeters outside behind her. The castle looked the same to her, but she felt different entering the spacious halls willingly. She was less nervous than she had been the last time, even though it had only been a couple of days since her first arrival in Eranox, and her first impression of the castle.

Margie led her through the corridors, leaving the strange welcoming committee behind them at the front doors, still playing their melody. She took her time winding through the long halls and up the stairs towards the room where Luna had stayed.

Margie opened the door quietly and Luna walked inside. The room was just as she had left it, her phone was still sitting on the night stand where she had abandoned it during her escape, though the necklace that she had left with it had been returned to her and hung around her neck.

"We've locked the windows Miss, I hope you don't mind." Margie flushed again as she closed the door over and hurried across the room to pull the curtains closed, covering the thick iron bars that now pressed against the glass preventing another escape attempt.

"Thank you Margie." Luna smiled, setting her school bag on the ground by the side of the bed, not sure where she should put it.

A trio of servants were waiting at the end of Luna's bed, fussing with a gown that they clearly expected her to wear.

"We will have to get you ready for Dinner now." Margie clicked, moving Luna's school bag across the room to the wardrobe, "They are having it early… *before curfew*…" She whispered loudly, letting Luna know that it was an unusual occurrence for dinner to be so early. "It's a *special* occasion…" She added, winking at Luna.

Luna tried not to sigh, knowing that it must have had something to do with her return and her new title of High Wizard, she was going to have to wear the dress.

Though it still felt strange, having others put her clothes on her, Luna knew that they were expecting to dress her in something more appropriate before she met the King.

Luna started to take off her Earth clothes, laying them on the end of the bed while the servants finished preparing the dress for her.

Luna turned to face them, tucking her arms through the gown that was being pulled over her head.

"Oh it looks lovely." Margie gushed as Luna's head popped out of the neck hole and the dress fell into place.

Luna felt the tug at her back as they began to tie it on her, she smiled as another servant reached for her hair.

"I see you've gotten your stone back." Margie smiled, "Glad to see it."

"Yes, Lucas brought it back for me." Luna answered politely.

"I had them put pockets in your dress." Margie stepped forward, showing Luna two slits in the seam. "I know you like to carry your *things*." She winked, reaching for Luna's phone on the night stand.

Luna accepted it, smiling as she tucked it into one of the pockets. Margie didn't need to know that the battery was dead and it didn't work in their world, though the pockets were a nice touch.

"Thank you." Luna smiled, it was all she could do while her dress was being tightened and her hair wrapped into a bun.

A moment later the tugging stopped and Margie put her hands to her face gleefully, "Well, turn, have a look." She pointed to the floor mirror behind Luna.

Luna spun, staring at herself in the mirror, her hair was poised at the top of her head, the dress rolling to her feet. It was a deep crimson with hints of burnt orange, it glimmered in the firelight, making it look like Luna herself was part of the flame.

"Very pretty." Luna smiled politely, knowing Margie was waiting for her reaction.

"Well then, off we go. Your escort should be waiting for you." Margie turned, opening the door a crack to check out into the hall. "And there he is." She swung the door open, curtsying to Lucas on the other side.

"Lady Blackwater." He held his hand out to her, a small smirk poised on his lips as he turned to face the hall.

He had changed too, he looked like a Prince from a fairy tale, his jacket matched Luna's dress.

Luna took his hand, nodding to the servants as she left the room, ready to play the part of the High Wizard if it would appease the King.

It was all so strange, she could have done the same job in jeans and a t-shirt, but she knew that Eranox was accustomed to their ways, so she played along as Lucas looped his arm in hers and led her through the castle standing tall like he was balancing a book on his head.

When they reached the Great Hall the King was waiting for them outside of the doors looking pensive. He bowed to

Luna as she approached, and she tried her best to curtsy while still walking to show her respect.

Lucas handed her arm over to the King and he turned leading her into the Great Hall where a feast was waiting.

"It is a pleasure to see you again Lady Blackwater." He gushed, pulling out a chair for her at the head of the table.

The room had grown silent, all eyes were on Luna as she sat in the chair at the center of the royal table, she glanced over to Lucas, sure that she had been placed in the wrong seat.

The King sat beside her, and Lucas placed himself on her other side, she was relieved that she would be able to whisper to him while they dined.

Servers entered the room, their footsteps echoing on the tile as the room remained focused on the head table. While the wine was poured the King rose, holding a goblet in his hand.

The servers finished their jobs and exited the room, the silence only growing.

"To the return of Lady Blackwater." The King announced, raising his glass in the air.

"To Lady Blackwater." The room chorused, taking a drink to Luna.

Luna felt her face growing red while the room stared at her, she nodded to the crowd, it seemed the only thing she could do.

They tipped their heads to her and finally turned back to their own tables, the servers returning a moment later with the first course.

Luna sat stiffly in her dress while the servers placed a soup at each place, waiting patiently as Lucas had told her for the King to begin the course.

The King sat silently, poised before the dish with a regal look about him, but he kept his hands in his lap. Luna turned to Lucas, he was staring at her, "You outrank him… you eat first." He hissed through a well-timed smile.

"Oh." Luna glanced at the King, he smiled at her as she reached for her spoon, dipping it into the soup.

She brought it to her lips and took a taste, and immediately heard the clatter of the others beginning their course.

"You should have told me." Luna leaned towards Lucas, trying not to draw too much attention, "Last time you said the King had to eat first…"

Lucas leaned closer, staring at his soup as he spoke, "You weren't officially the High Wizard then…" He mumbled, there was a tone of apology, but it was too late.

"Anything else I need to know?" Luna hissed.

"You'll be fine." Lucas went back to his soup quietly.

The meal passed quickly, there was a heaviness in the air that Luna knew meant talking was coming after the food was gone. It was so formal, though no one said a word to her, she knew that they were just waiting for the guests to leave so they could have their private conversation. Strange traditions that left Luna feeling edgy, she just wanted to ask a million questions, but she would have to wait.

As Luna set her dessert fork on the table the room clattered with the end of the meal. Lucas leaned towards her, "Stand and bow your head." He suggested, and Luna followed his instruction, listening as the rest of the room cleared.

She stood there for several minutes until she could hear the door closing and the room had gone quiet. When she looked up, Lucas and his father were standing on either side of her, heads bowed in the same way.

The King looked up, turning to her slowly.

"There is much we must discuss." He reached for her chair, pulling it out of her way. "Tonight I would like you to rest." He turned to Lucas, passing him a look, "The council will meet in the morning, we must ask that you remain in the castle for the night…" He seemed to have a knowing look in his eyes.

Luna felt sheepish, he was asking her not to run away again, and Lucas had told her that the curse had entered Eranox, so going outdoors after dusk was as dangerous as entering the Gateway itself.

"Thank you." Luna tipped her head, it seemed like the only thing she could say to keep the questions from spilling out. She would have to wait a while longer to get her answers.

"Lucas, will you take her to her room." The King stepped aside so Lucas could present his arm. Luna tucked her arm in his and let him guide her towards the door of the Great Hall, the King watched them as they left.

Luna kept herself poised until they were out of the Great Hall and back in the winding corridors of the castle interior.

"I thought he was going to tell me why I was here…" Luna whispered, waiting for Lucas to answer.

"Formalities Luna, I'm sorry, but you had to be presented as the High Wizard." Lucas sighed, "Now that we know your father isn't coming back, you are the High Wizard, officially." Lucas added, keeping his voice low.

"He had to appease the people, they will sleep happy tonight knowing they have you. Tomorrow we will have more time to discuss the curse." Lucas added.

"He's giving it another night to spread…" Luna reminded Lucas of the impending evening and the chaos that it was bringing.

"You wouldn't be able to do anything before dusk anyway." Lucas turned a corner, "It wouldn't be safe to try." He stopped before Luna's door.

"I guess this is it then." Luna looked at the door, already dreading a night in the strange room, "I'll see you in the morning."

"Send Margie if you need me." Lucas nodded his head, releasing Luna's arm, "And remember to stay inside." He added, opening the door for her.

"I will." Luna rolled her eyes, walking into the room.

Margie was waiting for her, a pot of tea rested on a table in the center of the room.

"Welcome back Lady Blackwater." Margie rose from her seat as the door closed behind Luna, she could hear Lucas' footsteps as he walked away.

"I will be staying with you for the night Miss, to keep an eye on things." Margie, stepped behind Luna and started to untie the corset of her dress, "I see that you have brought some of your own things." Margie pointed to the wardrobe across the room, "They've been pressed and hung for you." She tapped Luna on the arm.

Luna pulled her arms over her head and a moment later the dress was off. Margie carried it away to be hung.

"Do you mind if I wear my own night clothes?" Luna asked, hoping that her mom had packed her some pajama pants. She didn't want to be caught in a night dress again.

"Yes dear, that would be fine." Margie answered, fussing with the dress as she hung it.

Luna walked over to the wardrobe and opened it. She could barely contain a chuckle as she saw that all of the clothes had indeed been pressed and hung. Her pajama pants had a crease from being ironed, they looked pristine. It was almost a shame that Luna was going to wrinkle them up while she slept.

Quickly she dressed herself in her warm pajama pants and an old t-shirt that her mom had packed for her, she wondered what else had been in the school bag.

"Margie?" Luna poked her head out of the wardrobe, "Where are the other things from the bag?" She asked.

"Top drawer." Margie answered, coming to help, "Some strange stuff you brought too." She added, her eyes going wide as she pulled open the drawer for Luna.

Luna stared at the contents, some cookies, a few bottles of water, extra shoes and undergarments. And the notebook. Luna reached for the notebook and the pack of cookies.

"This is perfect." She stared at the book, tucking the cookies under her arm as she walked to the table where Margie had laid out the tea.

"What is it miss?" Margie seemed confused.

"Here." Luna set the cookies on the table and opened them, "Treats from Earth." She offered them to Margie with a smile, flipping open the notebook.

It was perfect, with her mom's notes and Margie there to help. Luna might be able to answer some of her own questions before she met the King in the morning.

She had time to be prepared.

Margie and Luna talked well into the night, and when Luna finally laid down to get some sleep, there were no nightmares waiting behind her closed eyes.

NINE

"Lady Blackwater…" The voice drifted into Luna's dreams, waking her. She opened her eyes and saw Margie standing beside the bed with a tray in her hands.

"Is it morning already?" Luna rolled over, trying to adjust to the strange surroundings. Light was spilling in through the window, Margie had already pulled back the curtains to invite the morning sun into the room.

"Yes dear." Margie smiled, "I've made you some tea." She rested the tray on the bedside table, "It's time to get you ready for breakfast." Margie pulled back Luna's blankets and stepped away to prepare her an outfit for the day.

The other servant girls had returned while Luna had been sleeping, she tried not to feel too strange about it, in Eranox that was the custom, and she would have to get used to it if she hoped to be able to help them.

She had a lot to get used to in Eranox.

Luna took a deep breath readying herself for the day and what was to come. She stepped from the bed and walked towards the center of the room, knowing that she was in for another uncomfortable dress.

Much to her surprise, the dress that they brought from behind the changing partition was much less fancy that she had been expecting, it seemed practical in comparison. It didn't have a corset, and easily slipped over her head after she removed her night clothes.

The fabric was soft and the dress was simple, it draped from her shoulders to the floor with little fussing. Margie had even added pockets into the seam, when Luna found them she couldn't help but smile. The dress was clearly made for her.

"It's perfect." Luna twirled, watching the fabric swirl at her feet. She still would have preferred jeans, but at least they weren't dressing her up like a Victorian Princess.

"And this." Margie appeared again from behind the partition, holding out a long cloak with symbols embroidered along the trim. "It's tradition for High Wizards." She smiled, helping Luna fasten the cloak over her shoulders with an ornate clasp at the collar.

She let the fabric fall, trailing from her shoulders to the ground. It was warm and comfortable, unlike the outfits she had been made to wear in Eranox previously. Though she wasn't sure that she could get away with wearing her running shoes under the dress, it wasn't as puffy as the others had been.

"By the door dear." Margie pointed, seeming to know what Luna was thinking.

Luna turned and looked, there was a pair of leather flats waiting for her. She crossed the room and slipped her feet in, surprised at how comfortable they felt.

"This is much better." Luna looked down at herself.

"Now your hair." Margie nodded her head, pulling Luna towards the mirror to see herself.

Luna's hair had gone wild while she had slept, the servants rushed in and within a few minutes they had it tamed again into a simple knot at the back of her neck.

Margie stepped back, giving Luna one last look over to be sure she was dressed properly.

"Are you ready Lady Blackwater?" Margie asked, watching Luna through the mirror.

"I think so." Luna turned plastering a smile on her face as she watched Margie, *this is it…* she thought to herself, hoping that she was ready for whatever Eranox needed her for.

"Now dear," Margie tucked her arm in Luna's while she slowly walked her towards the door, "Remember to be on your best." She whispered, leaning in so the other girls wouldn't overhear her, "Eranox needs you."

Luna turned to Margie, watching her for a moment, there was a pleading look in her eye. She was counting on Luna as much as anyone.

"Do you know someone out there?" Luna leaned in, keeping her voice low.

Margie looked down, shamefully, "Yes Miss." She whispered.

Luna reached for her hand, giving it a squeeze. "I will do my best." Luna whispered.

When Margie looked up, her eyes were watery, "Thank you Lady Blackwater, it's all I could ask." She bowed her head and opened the door.

Lucas was waiting on the other side.

He was dressed in a ruffled suit, the same embroidery running up his collar. Though Luna had been dressed more casual, she still matched Lucas in a subtle way.

"Breakfast Lady Blackwater." He tipped his head and held his arm out for her.

Luna looped her arm into his and followed him into the hall, trying to hold back the blind panic that was coursing through her veins. It had just struck her how many people were counting on her, how many families there were that thought she was going to save them and bring back their loved ones. All of Eranox, it *was* a lot to ask of a stranger from Earth; and she had already promised to do her best.

"Are you okay?" Lucas asked as Luna followed him stiffly down the corridor, suspecting that there was something on her mind.

Luna nodded, she didn't want Lucas to know how scared she really was, it wouldn't help anything.

Going back to Eranox was more than she had expected, there was so much that they were counting on her for and she was terrified that she was going to fail. She was one mistake away from letting an entire world down.

Lucas dropped the subject leading Luna through a door, "Breakfast." He announced taking a seat at a small table in the large castle room.

Luna sat across from Lucas, her stomach in knots as she tried to calm her nerves enough to eat something.

Breakfast that morning was a simple occasion. Luna and Lucas sat at a small table alone, eggs and bacon were brought out to them, or at least what *appeared* to be eggs and bacon. Luna couldn't tell and she was afraid to ask in case it was something different, at least it tasted the same to her.

"Did you sleep well?" Lucas asked, making small talk while he ate.

Luna nodded, Lucas stared at her.

"They didn't keep you up all night?" He sounded surprised.

"Who? Margie?" Luna wasn't sure what he was talking about, she had stayed up quite late talking to Margie, but she hadn't heard anyone else and Margie certainly hadn't kept her up by any means.

"No, no… Maybe your room is farther away…" Lucas shook his head, "They were in the woods last night, outside the castle by my room." He looked away, afraid to bring it up. "…The cursed…" He muttered, finally explaining what he had heard.

Luna paused, staring at her plate, the small appetite that she had mustered vanishing in an instant, "Was it bad?" She asked quietly.

"I don't think they got anyone." Lucas was quick to respond, he could see how guilty Luna must have felt, "But they were howling until dawn..." He added slowly, thoughtful almost.

"Wow, I'm surprised I didn't hear anything." Luna admitted, "They aren't exactly quiet."

"No they usually aren't." Lucas agreed smiling slowly, "I'm glad you were able to sleep, you'll be more alert when you meet the council." He added.

"What are they like?" Luna asked carefully, leaning forward in case Lucas thought to lower his voice. The thing about being in a castle, you never knew who was listening.

"Mostly boring." Lucas rolled his eyes, "I'm not sure what they really do in there to be honest, but nothing spectacular... at least until now." He tipped his head at Luna, an indication that they expected her to succeed.

"Are they nice though?" Luna imagined a stuffy room filled with teachers expecting her to pass a test, it didn't exactly seem inviting.

"Yeah, they're fine." Lucas got up from the table, "Are you going to be okay?" He asked, reaching for her hand.

"I think so." Luna answered, preparing herself to meet the council.

"You'll be great, trust me, it can't be that bad..." Lucas assured her, sort of, as he led the way back into the hall.

Soon Luna was being led to another chamber for the meeting with the council, two intimidating guards stood outside of the double doors watching as Luna and Lucas approached. She was sure that they were about to be turned away when the guard looked her over and nodded his head, reaching for the handle to open the door for her.

"You too Prince Lucas." The guard waited as Lucas hesitated outside.

"Really?" Lucas whispered, rushing forward to join Luna before the guard could change his mind. Lucas was surprised that they had allowed him to stay with Luna, though she was thankful that she wouldn't have to sit through the meeting alone. It was clear that Lucas was not expecting that he would be invited to this meeting and his father was making an exception for Luna's sake.

"Welcome Lady Blackwater." The King nodded, standing from his place at the head of the table.

Luna walked towards him into the chamber, the room was large with ornate carved wooden panels on all of the walls. The floor clicked even under her soft soled shoes as she walked. Down the center of the room ran a narrow table lined with high-backed chairs, the King stood at the far end watching as she and Lucas approached.

"I am glad you were able to join us today Lucas." The King smiled at his son, keeping his voice low, "I thought Lady Blackwater would feel more comfortable if she had some company her own age." He tipped his head, clearly he had already heard through the castle how Lucas had described the council as boring, though he didn't seem offended.

Lucas' cheeks flushed and he looked down at the floor, caught.

"Sorry father." Lucas mumbled.

"You weren't wrong." He chuckled, "Have a seat." The King turned his attention back to Luna.

Lucas showed her to her seat, at the right hand side of the King's chair that sat at the head of the table.

"Thanks." Luna settled herself and waited. The room was still empty, save the three of them, and she was sure that the council comprised of more people than just the King.

It was a short silence while they waited for the rest of the council to join them. Soon the far doors opened again and the room began to fill.

Men and women of Eranox, dressed in the strange attire that was considered the norm, their faces stoic as they prepared for the meeting.

Luna tipped her head to each to each of them as their eyes fell on her, the quiet excitement behind their eyes was apparent; they had a High Wizard again.

Lucas stood at his father's side as he waited for the table to fill, finally he slid into the last seat, the one across from Luna. He wouldn't be able to help her with the formalities without drawing too much attention. He tipped his head apologetically, for the meeting with the council she was on her own.

Slowly the council members settled into their seats at the table, their eyes lingering on Luna as they took their places. She could already feel their expectations of her as the new High Wizard weighing on her shoulders and did her best to keep her chin up so they wouldn't see how unprepared she really felt.

As the room finally fell silent the King leaned forward in his seat to address the council.

"Lady Blackwater, I want to thank you for joining us." He tipped his head to Luna and the room filled with murmurs of the council greeting her.

Luna tipped her head and looked down at her hands, trying to keep her composure before she looked back up at the King, hoping that he would continue so the room would stop staring at her.

The King smiled at Luna and continued, "It is unfortunate that your father, Sir Alec, was unable to return at this time." He turned to the rest of the table, "Lucas has informed me of the circumstances…" He shook his head sadly, looking at Luna apologetically.

"And what were the circumstances?" A Lady at the other end of the table inquired nervously, her eyes wide with curiosity.

"Madam Hawthorn," The King addressed her, "It appears that when Sir Alec departed with his family all of those years ago to find the cure… he was cursed himself before he ever left the Gateway."

The room filled with surprised gasps. Luna stared at her hands while the information echoed in the room, whispers running down the table just out of her earshot.

She could imagine what they were saying, what they were thinking, Sir Alec was supposed to be finding a cure; and he had been cursed. The notion sucked the hope right out of the room.

No one was coming back to save them.

"He was cursed?" Madam Hawthorn breathed, "This whole time…" She covered her mouth with her hand dramatically and Luna had to stop herself from rolling her eyes.

"How terrible." The man next to Luna stared at her as though he was waiting for her reaction.

Luna stayed silent, still staring at her hands, not sure if she was supposed to look sad. She had never known her father; to her the news of his curse explained his absence, it was more of a relief than anything.

The King cleared his throat, waiting for the chatter to die down before he carried on, "Despite the fact that we have lost Sir Alec to the curse, there is some good that has come of his prolonged absence." He watched the table as he spoke, waiting for their next reaction, "His child was protected and raised on Earth," All eyes turned to Luna, wide with surprise.

Apparently, despite the fact that she had already been introduced as a High Wizard, the notion that her father had been Sir Alec had some pull to it.

"And now Lady Blackwater is of age and has returned in her father's place." The King finished, tipping his head to Luna once again.

Luna looked up from her hands and found that the whole table was staring at her, their curiosity about her life on Earth was apparent, though no one dared to ask her what it was like.

"Welcome back Lady Blackwater." Madam Hawthorn nodded her head at Luna from her end of the table, regarding her as though she suddenly had immense significance.

Luna nodded back, "Thank you." She smiled politely, glancing to Lucas to see if she had handled the situation correctly. He smiled back at her, and she hoped that she was behaving properly for a council meeting.

"How delightful." Another woman at the table smiled, clapping her hands together.

"But where has she been this whole time?" Another man asked, watching the King for an answer.

"She has been on Earth." The King repeated, "and now she is here." He added, waiting for the chatter to die off again, as the attention turned back to him at his seat at the head of the table.

"Oh, how dreadful." Madam Hawthorn shook her head as though Luna had been trapped in a prison.

The King waited for her to finish, "Of course that is what brings us here today." He finally spoke again as Madam Hawthorn went silent, "We finally have a High Wizard, and we can try to restore the Kingdom…" He changed the subject swiftly, keeping the meeting going as he steered it towards his point.

"Sir Hawthorn, as many of you know, has devised a plan. Though up until this point we have not had a Wizard with the power required to put it in action." He gestured to a man at the other end of the table sitting next to Madam Hawthorn, presumably her husband.

"For Lady Blackwater, who has not been privy to our previous meetings, I shall quickly review the details so that we may proceed." He continued, skimming past the news that Luna had previously had no knowledge of Eranox in its entirety, though perhaps he himself didn't know how little Luna actually knew about their world and the Magic that she had coursing through her veins.

Luna dared a darting glance towards Lucas, but his face was unreadable. She didn't know if he had bothered to inform his father of her particular upbringing, and the lack of Eranoxian knowledge that it had contained.

The King turned in his chair slightly so he was facing Luna, though he kept his voice loud enough for the rest of the council to listen in as he brought Luna up to date, "Our Potion Master, Sir Hawthorn," He gestured to the man near the end of the table, "has spent the better part of the last ten years perfecting a potion that is believed to be able to separate the curse from its host." The King watched Luna's face as he spoke, "This potion has been tested with some success on smaller creatures, but thus far no one has been powerful enough to warrant a human test. With the power of a High Wizard, we believe that it will be able to lift the curse." The King gave Luna a knowing nod, telling her that this was the task they had brought her back for.

Though she was getting tired of all the head nodding and formalities, Luna nodded her head again in response, "That sounds promising." She replied, hoping that Lucas would have time to explain the potion and what they were expecting of her in more detail before she actually had to try the process. She glanced across the table and caught his eye. He smiled and nodded, reading her thoughts knowingly.

The King continued to stare at Luna, "The council has come to an agreement, that we shall test the spell on one participant first… to ensure that it will work for the masses." The King turned in his seat to address the rest of the council, his face growing stoic. "And given the situation, I believe that it would be best that we perform the first test on Sir Alec Blackwater." He suggested, gaining a collective gasp from the table. Even Luna felt her breath catch in her throat at the notion.

Madam Hawthorn cleared her throat and the room grew quiet again. "Given the circumstances, I am in agreement of the King's assessment." She smiled politely at the King, "To have Sir Alec cured of the curse would mean that we would have *two* High Wizards of the high bloodline that would be available to break the curse. I think it would be foolish to waste the Lady Blackwater's powers on anything else." She passed a stern glare up both sides of the table, daring anyone to disagree with her.

There was a chorus of nods and mumbles as the council fell into quiet agreement, even Luna could see the logic in the King's decision; Sir Alec was better suited for the job, all she had to do was cure him and then Eranox would be fine without her.

"Then it is settled." The King clapped his hands together, "Sir Alec shall be the first subject of the trial cure." The King turned to the man on the left of Madam Hawthorn, "Sir Hawthorn, we will require more of the potion, you are dismissed from the council to prepare."

Quietly the man rose from the table and excused himself from the room, though the rest of the council remained.

TEN

Lucas shifted uncomfortably in his seat as the door closed again, he looked up at Luna trying to catch her eye. He was trying to tell her something, his head shaking stiffly as though he wanted to warn her about what was about to happen, though she couldn't decipher the look on his face.

She wasn't sure what was going to happen next, but Lucas looked nervous, and she could tell that she wasn't going to be prepared for whatever it was that the King had planned.

Luna looked around the room, searching for a sign of what was coming, though the room remained the same; a table and a gathering of council members. If any of them knew what was about to happen, they hid it well.

The chatter swelled and then subsided again as the King waited for the room to become quiet before he continued talking, it seemed that the meeting of the council wasn't over just yet. Though Sir Hawthorn had departed there was more to come, and everyone seemed excited about what was about to happen next.

Finally the room fell silent again, the council members had turned to watch the King with rapt attention, ready for him to continue with the meeting. Luna could feel her heart racing, though she didn't know why just yet. Lucas looked concerned across the table from her, he wasn't watching his father. He had turned away to watch Luna, which wasn't helping her as she tried to stay calm.

The King cleared his throat, "Lady Blackwater," He turned towards Luna again and the council followed his gaze, "there was a time when we had hoped that your parents were out in the other worlds, finding a way to save us; a way to break the curse and bring us the aid that we so desperately needed to restore Eranox." His voice was low, many of the council members leaned forward in their seats to listen as he spoke, afraid to miss a single word.

Luna stared at the King, trying not to feel so uncomfortable, though she was sure that he was getting to something more important than her parents failed quest.

"Now," the King tipped his head sadly, "The curse is spreading again, and we are running out of time to make a change. We can no longer wait for the others to come and save us, we must do it ourselves or watch Eranox crumble beneath us."

The King rose from his seat, walking to a side door within the chamber that Luna hadn't even noticed before that moment. The council members turned in their seats to watch him.

"Sir Hawthorn may have finally found a way," The King continued, preparing himself for something, "But before we test his cure on your father…" He rapped on the side door three times, "We must know that you can work the magic."

He stepped back to the table quickly as the door began to open.

The strange side door opened and two Knights entered pulling a cage behind them. Inside was a small animal that Luna couldn't quite catch a good look at from her spot at the table, she stayed in her seat, as the council gasped with horror.

The room fell into absolute silence as the council members turned, staring at her as though they expected a display of her powers, as though she was there to entertain them.

Luna could feel her heart beating in her chest, she hadn't come prepared.

"What is that?" Luna hissed across the table at Lucas, trying her best to keep her composure, though she knew that she was losing it.

Lucas glanced her way, but he didn't answer. His face was stuck with a silent terror, and Luna knew that he was expecting something horrible was about to happen.

Instead, the King answered, "This," He gestured kindly to the cage as it rolled to a stop near the head of the table, "is a cat, Lady Blackwater. It is a creature that is often kept as a pet, normally docile and quite friendly when tamed." He smiled, turning to the room like he hadn't just explained what a cat was, clearly he didn't expect that Luna had encountered one before on Earth. "This cat was cursed quite recently, only a night ago."

He reached out for Luna's hand, and she rose from her seat, letting him guide her around the table towards the cage. "Would you be willing to try lifting the curse, if I guided you through it?" He asked kindly, his voice low, though Luna knew that the rest of the council was listening.

Luna knew that she would have to say yes, the rest of the council was watching her, this was the reason that she had come back to Eranox. She dared a glance back at Lucas, he looked surprised that they were asking her to try already. She hadn't even had time to get a proper explanation of what it was they were expecting her to do.

The King cleared his throat lightly, waiting for Luna's answer.

"Um, sure." Luna answered nervously.

"Thank you Lady Blackwater, we appreciate your cooperation. If this works, we will be able to lift the curse from Eranox, one victim at a time… until we are able to find another way…"

The King turned to the council, they had all stood from their seats and were watching with great interest.

"This is in no way ideal as the cure we had hoped for." The King spoke again, "But with Lady Blackwater's help, Eranox may survive and live to thrive again." He smiled at the council as they clapped with excitement.

The pressure was building in the room, and the longer the King spoke the more riled up the council became, they clearly had high expectations and Luna was starting to feel like the room was shrinking around her. There was no escape from it, there was no more time to prepare herself. Even Lucas looked scared for her, and in that moment she wondered what was going to happen to her if she failed.

What would the council think if she wasn't unable to lift the curse? Would she get to go home? Would they let her leave alive? For a moment she wasn't quite sure.

"Are you ready?" The King whispered, not waiting for Luna to answer.

He reached beneath his cloak and procured a bottle from his waist, "First we must release the potion onto the creature, it helps separate the curse from the being." He instructed, handing Luna the small vial."

Luna looked down at the small glass vial in her hand, the thick murky liquid inside felt warm through the glass, "I just pour it over?" She asked quietly, releasing the cork.

"Yes." The King answered, staying back while Luna approached the cage.

The scent from the vial smelled putrid, like it had gone moldy while it had been bottled up. She wondered how long the small vial had been kept, waiting for a High Wizard to use it, she wondered if it was even still any good.

She gripped the vial in her hand as she took another step towards the cage, trying to keep her hand from shaking so she didn't spill the precious liquid before she was ready.

The cat seemed normal, perhaps because it was daytime and the effects of the curse were more prominent at night. The small creature sat still in the cage, staring ahead as though no one were in the room with it. It's casual blankness was a symptom that Lucas had explained to her in the Gateway. There was no doubt in her mind that the cat was cursed, it didn't even blink as she approached it.

She took another step towards the cage, breathing slowly to calm her nerves as she reached the gilded bars that contained the still cat. Slowly she reached up and tipped the vial over the cage, the thick liquid seemed to float down in a cloud, enveloping the cat as it poured out of the small bottle.

Luna stepped back and handed the empty vial and cork back to the King, "And what do I do next?" She asked, keeping an eye on the cat in the cage, it still hadn't moved a muscle, though the potion hovered over it like a second skin. She was surprised that the cat wasn't reacting to it at all.

"Here." The King tucked the spent vial away and reached for her hand again, "I want you to *feel* the power, I will guide you through it." He whispered only to her, drowning out the rest of the council so she could concentrate, "Feel the cat's life force, focus on it, you will know where the curse is." He explained.

"Okay." Luna nodded, reaching her other hand out towards the cage, she closed her eyes as she concentrated, trying to find the cat in her mind.

"Once you have the cat, feel the curse, feel the curse lifting from the cat out of its body." The King's voice drifted into Luna's mind. "Push it out with your power."

Surprisingly, Luna could feel it. Like a rush of fire coursing through her veins, the magic flowed through her. She imagined the cat, so frail and still, its spirit separating from the darkness that had taken it over. She could see in her mind as the dark began to separate, the burden of the curse lifting. The ashy cloud hovered over the cat, waiting for her next command.

"What do I do with the curse now?" Luna asked, squeezing the King's hand in hers to be sure that he was still there to help her. "It's out, but what do I do with it now?" She held her eyes closed, afraid to let go of the curse, afraid that if she did it would find another host.

"Dissolve it Lady Blackwater, send it back to the stars." The King's voice was even and calm, he still held her hand firmly rooting her in the room.

Luna twisted her palm, imagining the swell of darkness burning up into ash and disintegrating into nothing. When she felt that it was all gone, she opened her eyes.

She was dizzy, the King held her as she swayed, trying to stay on her feet as the room around her twisted.

"Bring Lady Blackwater a chair." The King's voice sounded like it was underwater, though his hand was still holding hers, she gripped it tightly afraid of letting go.

Lucas appeared beside her, gently helping her sit down in the chair that had been set behind her. "Are you okay?" He whispered, leaning in close, his face swaying before Luna.

"Did it work?" Luna asked, turning her head to look at the cage again as the nausea began to fade.

The cat was staring at her, it's green eyes were curious. It stretched and yawned, pawing at the bars of the cage before it began to pace, suddenly alive again.

"Oh my, it worked." Madam Hawthorn exclaimed, stepping closer to have a look at the specimen in the cage, "Very impressive Lady Blackwater." She smiled at Luna with excitement.

Luna tried to smile but she could tell by the look on Madam Hawthorns face that it had come out as more of a grimace.

"Oh dear, you look pale, are you alright?" Madam Hawthorn leaned forward hovering in Luna's face.

"She'll be okay." Lucas answered gently, stepping forward to edge Madam Hawthorn out of the way.

The King clapped his hands together, drawing the attention back away from Luna. "As you can see, the cat has been relieved of the burden of the curse." He waved his hand towards the cage and the gaze of the council followed, "The cure that Sir Hawthorn has been perfecting has finally been tested successfully and we can move forward with a cure for Eranox."

"And now Lady Blackwater will cure Sir Blackwater?" Madam Hawthorn asked, not ready to lose all of the attention quite yet.

The King chuckled, "I do believe Lady Blackwater could use a rest, and Sir Hawthorn will require some time to produce a larger batch of the potion."

"What's next then?" Luna asked quietly, wondering just how much longer it would be before she was able to get that rest that the King had mentioned.

"The cat shall remain guarded through this nightfall." The King advised, tipping his head to the two Knights who stood silently behind the cage before he turned back to the council, "We wouldn't want to make any mistakes here, we need to wait until the time of the curse is upon us to ensure that it has been fully lifted from the cat."

The room nodded in agreement.

"At this time I think we should adjourn for the day." The King turned back to the Knights, "Guard this cage, and alert me if there are any changes." He advised them, stoically the two Knights nodded as they began to take the cage out of the room and into the side chamber where the cat had been kept before Luna had lifted its curse.

Slowly the council exited the room through the main doors, leaving Luna with the King and Lucas.

It was time for her to get some answers.

ELEVEN

The King waited in silence until the doors had closed before he spoke again. As the last member of the council finally departed and the Knights closed the doors back over from the other side the King finally turned to face Luna again.

"You did well on the test." He smiled, clearly relieved that Luna had been as powerful as he had hoped. "How did you feel?" He asked, watching carefully for a sign that she might not be up to curing something larger.

"It was strange." Luna admitted, "But I think I could get the hang of it."

The King looked to Lucas for an explanation, not sure of Luna's Earthly slang.

"She thinks she could do it again." Lucas repeated.

"I am glad to hear it." The King continued to smile, "If the cat remains unchanged through the night our next step is to capture Alec Blackwater and have him cured." The King repeated the information he had mentioned earlier in case Luna hadn't understood, "Once he is cured, he will be able to assist you in healing Eranox from this curse. There will be less pressure on you once the true High Wizard is restored." He reminded Luna, his face pensive.

"Once he is cured I could go home and let my mom know how things are going?" Luna asked, checking Lucas for a reaction. She wasn't sure if Lucas had mentioned anything to his father about Luna returning home.

"I don't see why not, for a quick visit." The King nodded, "But we would still need you here to accelerate the cure." He added, reminding Luna that she would still be needed once Alec returned as High Wizard.

"How will they capture him while he is still cursed?" Luna wondered aloud. The Gateway was a dangerous place and he could be anywhere inside of it.

"The Knights are already searching for him. Two teams are scouring the Gateway during the day while it is safe." He sounded like he had it all planned out, "When he is found, he will be caged in the Gateway and only transported here to the castle when we are ready to have him cured." He answered plainly.

"So there is no chance that he could escape and spread the curse in Eranox..." Luna continued, seeing the logic in the King's plan.

"Precisely." He nodded.

"We will still be needing you for a few days." Lucas reminded her, "Are you prepared to stay? Until Alec Blackwater is able to take over at least..." He asked offering Luna the out that he had promised her.

"I think that I will be okay to stay for a few days." Luna agreed, hoping that her mom wouldn't be too worried about her back on Earth, "But I should probably go back to let my mom know I'm okay, once Alec is ready." She added.

"That is agreeable." The King nodded, "Now we wait," He clapped his hands together, signaling the end of their discussion. "I am sure that Lucas has some time to show you around, you should get to know more about Eranox while we wait for Sir Alec to be captured." The King smiled, a twinkle in his eye as he ushered the two of them towards the door.

Lucas shook his head, his cheeks flushed with embarrassment, "Okay father, we get the point, you have things to do and need us out of your way." He reached towards the door.

As he opened it a young girl fell into the room.

"Oof." She collected herself off of the floor. She had clearly been listening with her ear pressed against the door and been caught off guard when Lucas had opened it. Her cheeks were red as she looked up at Lucas and the King guiltily. "Sorry..." She dusted her dress off and reached for Lucas' hand to pull herself back up to her feet.

"Ezzie." Lucas chided, "You know that you aren't supposed to be here." He led her from the room before the King could say a word.

Luna followed, wondering who the strange girl was and why she had never seen her before.

"Is that her?" Ezzie asked, looking over her shoulder at Luna, "*Lady Blackwater?*" She hissed, giggling under her breath.

"Yes, Ezzie." Lucas answered, rolling his eyes, "Her name is Luna, she is here to help"

"Oh, that's a pretty name." Ezzie squealed, peeking over Lucas' shoulder again to stare.

"What were you doing down here Ezzie?" Lucas finally stopped walking a few paces from the council room doors, lowering his voice, "You know you aren't allowed at the council meetings... you shouldn't have been listening..."

"You aren't either." Ezzie answered, crossing her arms over her chest, "Why were *you* allowed to go this time?" She asked in a sing-song voice.

Lucas sighed, glancing back at Luna like he hoped that she hadn't heard, "Father asked me to come to the meeting, so I could help Luna..." He answered, looking at his feet like he had been caught.

"You aren't normally there?" Luna asked, feeling kind of sheepish watching Lucas and Ezzie talk about her while she was standing right there.

"Oh, sorry Luna." Lucas turned to the young girl at his side, "This is my sister, Ezmerelda, or Ezzie." He introduced the strange girl who was still staring at Luna. "And no, I am not usually privy to the council meetings, not until I am granted the title of King in waiting…" He added as though he wanted Luna to know that one day he *would* be privy to the meetings. "I was asked to sit in so you would feel more comfortable…"

"Oh." Luna tried to hide her surprise. She hadn't known that Lucas had a sister he had never mentioned much about his family while he was on Earth, and Luna hadn't met her during her last short stay. Though she could see why Lucas wasn't normally at the council meetings, they were boring and formal and it seemed that everything had already been decided before the meeting had even begun, there was no point in dragging him through the meetings until he had a reason to need to know what was going on.

Ezzie stared at Luna and curtsied, "It is a pleasure to meet you Lady Blackwater." She tipped her head formally.

Luna stared at Lucas, suddenly more uncomfortable, she wasn't sure how she was supposed to greet a Princess, "You can call me Luna, really…" She smiled at Ezzie, not sure if she should curtsy back, "It's nice to meet you too, I didn't know that Lucas had a sister…" She admitted passing Lucas another look.

Lucas blushed, "She wasn't a part of my story on Earth…" He tried to explain, "I didn't tell you about her because… you couldn't meet her, at least not on Earth… I would have told you about her eventually…" He tried to defend his choice to omit his sister's existence from his life but it was apparent that Ezzie was offended that he hadn't mentioned her.

"You *didn't* tell her that you had a sister!" She huffed, crossing her arms again, "No wonder she ran off…" Ezzie rolled her eyes, "What *did* you tell her?" She asked quite pointedly.

"We were kind of on the run when she found out about this place…" Lucas reminded his sister, "I didn't really have time to give her my whole family history, she didn't even know that Eranox existed…"

"Didn't even know about Eranox?" There was a twinkle in Ezzie's eyes, and Luna wasn't sure if it was because she had found out something she wasn't supposed to know, or if she was planning something mischievous.

"Don't give me that look." Lucas stared at her, clearly knowing which of the two it was that had caused her eyes to spark.

"If she doesn't know about Eranox…" Ezzie smiled, "Well, *I* can change that…" She turned to Luna, "You need the grand tour. The *good* one without someone boring trying to ruin all the fun." She shot a look at Lucas. "Come on, you are going with me today." She insisted reaching for Luna's arm. "You can stay here and keep pretending that you don't have a sister." Ezzie smirked at Lucas as she started tugging Luna down the hall, leaving him standing there looking confused.

TWELVE

"There is so much that I *need* to show you." Ezzie let go of Luna's hand as they turned a corner, another corridor spread out ahead of them, "Oh, you are going to *love* Eranox." She giggled leading the way.

"How on Earth did I not know that Lucas had a sister?" Luna chuckled, Ezzie sure had a way of making her presence known.

"That's just it." Ezzie frowned, "You were on Earth, and I wasn't allowed to go with him…" She trailed off, a slight bitterness in her words. "Next time you go back, I want to go with you." She whispered, looking over her shoulders like she was afraid of being heard.

"That would be interesting." Luna answered politely, imagining Ezzie, a Princess from another world, trying to fit in in River Falls. It would be amusing at the very least.

Ezzie kept walking, finally reaching the front doors to the castle. She swung her arms out, the doors following her command and opening wide, allowing the bright sunlight to enter the castle.

"Come on." She danced down the steps, waiting for Luna at the bottom, "You've got a whole city to see."

There was a carriage waiting outside the front doors as though it were expecting them. The strange horses that she had seen when she had returned with Lucas were waiting impatiently, their wings ruffling as they tapped their hooves on the stones.

Ezzie however, walked right past the carriage, waving it off, "We go on foot." She announced, "There is so much you cannot see from a carriage." She turned back to Luna, "Are you ready?" She asked excitedly.

Luna looked out at the castle walls, remembering her first trip on foot through Eranox, "Sure, I'm ready…" She answered, following Ezzie towards the castle gates.

Ezzie walked with a hop in her step, so lightly that Luna was sure she was going to bounce right into the sky. She was petite and smiled easily, it was hard to believe that Eranox was cursed with all of the cheer that radiated off of her.

"So, what is it like?" She asked, turning to Luna with a curious eye, "Being a High Wizard that is…" She clarified when Luna didn't answer right away.

"Strange." Luna answered, there was no other way to describe it. She had felt the fire rolling through her blood, felt the curse with her power and burned it in her mind. She hadn't yet found a way to describe how it felt to her other than strange.

"I'm just getting used to my power." Ezzie admitted, "I just turned sixteen last moon, and finally started my training." She flicked her hand and a small flame appeared.

"Well Happy Birthday …" Luna smiled, wondering what was involved in the training that Ezzie had just begun. "Any chance you could show me some of the things you've learned?" She asked, wanting to watch how Ezzie used her powers so she could figure out where to start herself.

Ezzie's eyes lit up, "Really?" She stopped walking a few paces before the gate to the city.

"Yeah, I would love to see what you've learned." Luna wasn't sure if anyone in Eranox was supposed to know that she hadn't been trained, so she kept it to herself, hoping that Ezzie wouldn't pick up on it.

"Here." Ezzie turned, pointing to a shrubbery, "Watch this." She scrunched her face up, her hand extended towards the plant. Slowly it began to smoke, the branches heating up, though it wasn't enough to start a fire.

"Cool." Luna smiled, watching Ezzie, she seemed to be out of energy.

"It takes a lot out of you…" She huffed, "I'm still trying to get used to it."

Luna knew the feeling, she still felt drained from the test spell on the cat. She could only imagine how much energy it was going to take to lift the curse from a full sized human.

"We should get going." Ezzie pulled herself together, turning back to the gates, "I've got a lot to show you, and curfew is so early these days." She sighed.

"Curfew?" Luna asked.

"Two hours before dusk." Ezzie impersonated someone that Luna didn't know.

"That's pretty strict," Luna commented, "but that curse is very dangerous, so I'm sure it's for your own safety." She reminded Ezzie, she knew that Lucas wouldn't want his sister putting herself in danger, and she had seen first-hand what happened at night.

"Oh, I know." Ezzie rolled her eyes as they stepped through the gates. The guards nodded to her and Luna as they passed. "It's just so frustrating…" She trailed off apologetically.

Without having to say anything, Luna knew that it was her fault that the curfew had been put in place.

"What should we do first?" Ezzie's tone changed as the gates closed behind them and they entered the bustling streets of Eranox.

Luna stared out at the crowd, some of the pedestrians had stopped to look, realizing that the Princess and the High Wizard were in the streets seemed to cause them some alarm. They rushed to bow and quickly scattered, whispers filling the street as the crowd grew, peering at them from a distance.

"Hilda?" Ezzie called to no one in particular.

A girl appeared from behind them, startling Luna, she was one of the servants from the castle.

"Yes Miss?" She tipped her head to both of them.

"We would like a lunch in the square, and I think I would like to take Lady Blackwater to see the Potion Master." She smiled thoughtfully.

"Is that all?" Hilda asked, tipping her head to the side to wait for Ezzie's answer.

"For now." Ezzie smirked, reaching for Luna's hand, "Come on Lady Blackwater, we have a lot to see." She pulled Luna into the street and led the way through the watching crowd, seemingly unfazed by their stares.

It was a different route than the one she had taken with Lucas through Eranox on her first visit. Though the street looked much the same, the stores were quite different, and the houses were much stranger.

"This is row Seven." Ezzie caught the look on Luna's face, "Leads out to the Gateway like all the others, but row Seven is my favorite place to look. It has the prettiest gardens and the nicest shops." She took a deep breath, "Plus the square between Seven and Eight is a beautiful little place to take a meal." She added wistfully, "You'll love it."

"So where are we going first?" Luna looked around at all the shops lining the street, there were fewer houses in row Seven than there had been on the street Lucas had led her down towards the castle on her first visit. It seemed that Ezzie had taken her to the shopping district in town.

Though she still didn't know much about Eranox she was starting to feel a little excited about being able to look around and learn some things first hand. It was much better than relying on her mother's notes from the Eranox she had left eighteen years ago.

"Potion Master." Ezzie answered, "Just up ahead." She led the way down the busy street, though the people seemed to part for them, watching with curious eyes as the Princess and the High Wizard passed them by on the street. It was clearly a sight that they didn't see often.

Ezzie turned towards a large storefront, it seemed to take up a whole block with its glass windows and signs. Painted on the front window, in what looked like gold, were the words *Potion Master* in large elegant letters that were full of swoops and spirals.

Ezzie pushed the door open, walking inside and taking a deep breath of the air inside of the shop. "Can you smell it?" She turned, whispering to Luna as she followed her inside, "It *smells* like power." She turned away, walking towards the first of many shelves.

"There is so much stuff in here." Luna reached for a jar, turning it to read the label, "Sage…" She stared at the contents, trying to figure out if it looked like the sage from Earth, or if Eranox had a different variety.

"This is where they keep the more common ingredients." Ezzie explained, looking at the shelf that Luna was staring at like it was too boring for her to bother with, "Anything more… potent… is kept towards the back." She lowered her voice mischievously.

"And these are all used to make potions?" Luna tucked the jar back onto the shelf.

"Some are used for common things, cleaning, cooking, but yes, they are all ingredients one might need for a potion." Ezzie's eyes lit up again, "Come with me." She looked over her shoulder again, like she was about to do something that she wasn't supposed to do. She lowered her voice, "They also carry ready-made potions…" She whispered.

She slipped out of the aisle and crept towards the back of the shop, slipping behind a curtain that blocked the area from view.

Luna was sure that they weren't supposed to be there, but she followed Ezzie, her curiosity getting the better of her.

"These are all potions?" Luna stared at the shelves, they were filled with different shaped glass vials and jars, some similar to the one that had held the potion she had used to lift the curse on the cat at the castle.

She was afraid to touch the bottles to see what was written on them, though Ezzie didn't seem to have the same concern. "Look at this one." She reached for a twisted bottle, the cork at the top had turned a glowing green.

"You probably shouldn't touch that…" Luna backed up a step, she wasn't sure what was in the bottle, but she also didn't want to find out. Some of the potions were probably very dangerous, there was a reason that they were kept away behind the curtain.

"Oh, you're just like Lucas…" Ezzie tisked, tucking the bottle back onto the shelf as she rolled her eyes at Luna.

"You aren't supposed to be back here." A voice whispered, seeming to come from nowhere.

Luna turned, trying to find where it had come from, but Ezzie didn't seem to be alarmed.

"Where are you hiding Jack?" Ezzie crossed her arms, though there was a smirk on her face and a twinkle in her eyes.

Luna watched her with amusement, wondering where Jack was hiding, and how he and Ezzie knew each other.

A moment later a young boy, about Ezzie's age, hopped down from the top of one of the shelves. He had been perched on the top watching them.

He looked disheveled, like he had stepped out of an old book about a boy who lived in the woods and liked to fish. His feet were bare and his pants were ripped at the bottom and barely covered his ankles, but he had the same mischievous twinkle in his eye that Ezzie had in hers.

"You two are friends?" Luna asked, watching as the boy stared.

Ezzie looked up, her cheeks blushing like she had forgotten that Luna was there.

"Yes." She smiled, putting on the airs, "Jack, this is Lady Blackwater, the new High Wizard."

Jack turned, standing tall as he mocked Ezzie's posture, "A pleasure to meet you Lady Blackwater." He bowed deeply, nearly hitting his head on a shelf.

"You can call me Luna." Luna rolled her eyes, knowing that Jack was the rebellious type and wasn't likely to treat her any differently than any other person, which she was perfectly fine with.

"That would be much easier." He smirked, turning back to Ezzie, "What are you looking for today?" He asked, poking at a bottle on the bottom shelf as though he were trying to guess.

"Nothing, this time…" Ezzie giggled, "I'm just showing Lady Blackwater around Eranox." She lowered her voice, but Luna could still hear her, "She's new here." Ezzie whispered, winking.

Jack peeked over his shoulder at Luna, giving her a long once over that was quite uncomfortable. Then he turned back to Ezzie, "She the one from Earth?" He whispered with curiosity.

"She is." Ezzie answered, the twinkle back in her eye again.

Jack turned to face Luna, looking her over again, "You from Earth?" He asked.

"Yes." Luna answered.

"Is there magic there?"

"No, I don't think there is." Luna wasn't really sure.

"And you're the High Wizard now?" He continued.

"Apparently." Luna crossed her arms, waiting for Jack to get to the point, there was clearly something that he actually wanted to know.

"The one who cured the cat?"

"How did you hear that?" Luna asked, wondering how fast word spread in Eranox, it couldn't be as bad as River Falls.

"My dad's the Potion Master." He answered smugly.

"Sir Hawthorn?" Luna asked to be sure that it was the same man that she had met at the council.

"One in the same." Jack nodded proudly, "I hear that you get to cure the *real* High Wizard tonight…" His smile was growing.

Luna didn't answer, it was clear that Jack knew enough.

"What's Earth like?" Jack finally asked.

Ezzie peered over his shoulder at Luna, she seemed to be wondering the same thing, but had been too proper to ask straight out.

Luna chuckled, "I don't know enough about Eranox to really compare," She admitted, "But it's like Eranox without magic, and maybe a hundred years in the future." She looked up at the fire lit sconces, wondering when Eranox would learn about electricity.

"A hundred years in the future?" Jack's eyes went wide, "You live in the clouds?" He asked, serious.

Luna wasn't sure how to answer, it was clear that his idea of the future was quite different than what she had been trying to explain. "We just… Earth I mean, they learned to advance without magic…" Luna tried to think of a way to explain it, "It's very different from here, but kind of the same…"

"That's it?" Jack sounded disappointed at her explanation of the other world.

"Maybe you can see it one day, once the Gateway is safe again." Luna suggested, "I could show you around." She glanced towards Ezzie, "You too." She added.

Jack stuck out his hand, "It's a deal then." He nodded his head, accepting her offer.

Luna reached out, shaking his hand, the promise that she would show him Earth one day hanging in the air.

Something banged from the back of the store. Jack lost his smile immediately.

"You should get out of here before my father comes back out for more ingredients." He suggested, glancing over his shoulder as another loud crash sounded from the back.

Ezzie's eyes went wide, "Come on Lady Blackwater, we should go." She whispered.

"It was nice meeting you Jack." Luna nodded to the boy and followed Ezzie back through the curtains towards the front of the shop.

"That was a close one." Ezzie whispered, opening the door and darting back into the street, "Sir Hawthorn gets very cranky if he catches you in the back without an appointment." She twirled her dress, catching it on a breeze.

"So, how long have you known Jack?" Luna asked, giving Ezzie a knowing look.

Ezzie blushed, "His parents are both on the council," She averted her eyes, "The maids have been watching us during council meetings since we were babies…" She turned to the street, "Come on, I'm sure lunch is ready." She changed the subject, hurrying though the parting crowd towards the court that Luna could only presume was up ahead.

Ezzie slowed up enough for Luna to catch up to her as they turned a corner into the square. It was a large space between two buildings that linked row Seven and row Eight, as Ezzie had already explained. Though it didn't seem to receive much in the way of sun, it was still a bright and beautiful place.

Blue candles hung from the chandeliers that draped down from an upper balcony that covered the space. And somehow, even in the dark shadows of the buildings beside it, the gardens thrived.

Much like the castle, the flowers were unrecognizable to Luna, though that didn't tarnish their beauty in the slightest. Deep reds and glowing oranges sprouted from the lush greenery.

It looked like a magical place.

"This way." Ezzie reached for Luna's hand again, guiding her to a staircase at the side of the square.

Luna followed her up, the stair spiraled until they reached the balcony and all of Eranox laid out beneath them.

They were at least three stories up, in Luna's Earth measurements that is. She could see the castle more clearly from their height and distance. She could finally see it for what it really was.

The beautiful arching white stones gleamed in the sun, a pillar of time in Eranox, and breathtaking to see from such a vantage.

"Pretty, isn't it?" Ezzie tried to catch Luna's attention, "Look the other way." She suggested.

Luna stared at the castle for a moment longer before she turned to see what Ezzie was trying to show her.

The Gateway.

It was strange to see it in the day, from such a height that the tops of the walls were visible, twisting and turning to create the maze. Luna imagined how many people had stood on that very balcony and tried to find the way through the Gateway with their eyes. It seemed much easier when you couldn't see what was below, and what was hiding between the walls.

For the first time Luna could see past the Gateway, into the world beyond the barrier. It was all forest as far as the eye could see, the trees were the colors of autumn, though the leaves looked fresh and vibrant.

"What is out there?" Luna asked quietly, not taking her eyes off of the world beyond the maze.

"The rest." Ezzie answered, "More of the world, less of the Kingdom."

"What?" Luna didn't understand.

"This." She pointed to the city. "This is the heart of Eranox, the Kingdom itself." Ezzie tried to explain, "Out there is more of Eranox, different villages, but they are all below the Kingdom, just common folk."

"Do they have magic?" Luna wondered.

"Yes, but not like the High Wizards, not like the Royals." She sounded proud to be included.

"Are they cursed?" Luna whispered, afraid to hear the answer.

"I don't know." Ezzie turned towards Luna, a curious expression on her face. "They used to send word by Gwin sometimes, but only my father really knows."

"There is an entire world out there, and no one knows what happened to it?" Luna was surprised, she had thought that Eranox was just a city.

It made sense though, Earth was bigger than one city, but it was still a lot to process.

"Or they could be safe from it." Ezzie reminded her, "The Gateway has been sealed off for eighteen years…"

"It only takes one of them to spread the curse…" Luna muttered under her breath. Suddenly she needed to know how the rest of Eranox, the world outside of the Kingdom, was surviving.

Or if they had been cursed too.

If the curse had spread to them, if there was only a handful of un-cursed left, her mother was right, Eranox was beyond repair.

"Lady Blackwater, Princess Ezmerelda, lunch is served." A servant appeared at Luna's elbow, gesturing to a small table that had been set in the center of the balcony for the two of them.

"Thank you." Luna smiled, hiding her inner panic as she played the part of Lady Blackwater and stepped towards the table.

She was finding it much easier to separate Lady Blackwater from herself when she pretended that she was playing a part in a play, letting the *real* her remain intact beneath the facade. It just made it easier for her to cope with the new expectations and no one seemed to notice that it was an act.

Ezzie slipped into a chair across from her, staring out at the Gateway with a curious expression on her face, "Do you really think it's cursed out there, that the Kingdom is all that is left?" She whispered, uncaring that the servants were currently placing food before her, to Ezzie they didn't seem to matter.

Luna bit her tongue, waiting for the servants to leave before she answered. She knew how rumors spread, and it all started with a waiting ear.

"Thank you." Luna tipped her head at the server as he placed a bowl before her.

When he had finally departed Luna leaned forward, lowering her voice, "I don't know. But you can't talk so openly about it, servants talk too…" Luna reminded her, glancing over her shoulder, she was sure that they were just around the corner, trying to listen.

Ezzie seemed surprised, "I didn't even consider…" She looked thoughtful, "All this time…" She shook her head. "You are right though, this is a more serious matter. It can wait." She dipped her spoon into her soup, making it clear to Luna that the strange meal protocol only affected life in the castle.

Luna smiled and stared out at the city of Eranox, watching life on the bustling streets while her food grew cold. She was far less than hungry, her mind was somewhere else, worried about another million things. It was hard to even consider eating given the circumstances.

THIRTEEN

When lunch was finally over, Luna and Ezzie stayed up on the balcony, watching over Eranox.

There was still so much of the city that they couldn't see, even from up high on the balcony. It would take Ezzie months to show Luna everything that Eranox had to offer, but for a first trip the young Princess was certainly trying to cover as much as she could into one day.

There were places that Luna had never heard of before, sports fields for games that she couldn't imagine. It was like she was relearning everything she had ever known, but on a new world, her mom had been right, even with the cheat sheets she had been given, it would take a long time to understand Eranox and how it worked.

"And over there," Ezzie pointed, "Is the school. Lucas said you have schools on Earth." She added, waiting for Luna to confirm the rumor.

"Yeah, that's where Lucas and I met." Luna recalled.

"So, are you two… betrothed or anything?" Ezzie asked slyly.

Luna laughed, "Just friends." She answered, "And even that I'm not sure of."

"Really?" Ezzie sounded surprised, "Lucas talked about you a lot when he was traveling." She added, "He was really excited for you to come to Eranox for real, he even asked for an extension, because he like it there so much…" Ezzie giggled.

"Is *that* why he asked for it?" Luna laughed, "We do have really good snacks on Earth, totally horrible for you, but delicious." Luna smiled.

"Why don't you think you're friends?" Ezzie tipped her head, still staring at the city.

"It's just complicated…" Luna shrugged her shoulders, "He knew who I was, and I didn't… we didn't meet by accident…" She couldn't really put it into words, but Ezzie turned, her eyes boring into Luna, she looked like she understood.

Ezzie didn't say another word about Lucas after that, she just pointed out over Eranox, showing Luna where all the interesting places were hidden.

"Lady Blackwater? Princess Ezmerelda?"

Luna turned, Ezzie's maid was standing behind them looking quite sheepish.

"Yes?" Ezzie turned away from the view.

"Curfew is coming, they have sent a carriage for you." She curtsied politely.

Luna looked over the balcony, watching as the strange carriage came into view, turning itself around in the square to carry them back to the castle.

"Thank you." She answered before Ezzie could, "We should be going." She reached for Ezzie's hand.

Ezzie followed her back down the winding stairs and into the waiting carriage. It was hard to believe that the day had passed so quickly, Luna was just getting to know Ezzie, and a lot more about Eranox.

"Back to the castle." Ezzie grumbled as the carriage lurched forward down the street.

"I'm here for a couple of days." Luna reminded her, "We can go exploring again tomorrow." She suggested.

"You would?" Ezzie smiled. "There is *so* much more you need to see." She was already making plans.

"I'm in." Luna smiled

"Oh, you have *so* much more to learn."

"Like, do those *alicorn,* the ones pulling the carriage, Do they really fly?" Luna asked, staring out the window as the city of Eranox passed her by.

Ezzie looked out the window too, "I don't know, I've never seen one try…" She smiled with excitement.

Within minutes they were back at the castle, exiting the carriage by the massive front doors.

Margie was waiting for her, just inside of the castle, in a hurry to bustle her away.

"I'll see you at dinner." Luna waved at Ezzie and followed Margie down the hall.

"Did you have fun in the city?" Margie asked, opening Luna's door to reveal a new dress waiting for her.

"It was beautiful." Luna smiled, helping as they tried to dress her for dinner, "I didn't realize it was so big." Luna gushed, remembering her warning to Ezzie, she didn't inquire about the world outside of the Kingdom while Margie was listening.

"I'm glad you had fun." Margie smiled, "But you are nearly late for dinner." She chided, "That Princess sure knows how to cut things close." She tisked, as though Ezzie had a reputation for being late that Luna should have known about.

"She's a lovely girl." Luna smiled, checking herself in the mirror. "Thank you." She turned to Margie.

"Yes Miss." Margie nodded, poking her head out the door and into the hall, "Speaking of late…" She muttered.

"Who's late?" Luna asked.

"Oh, no one dear. Your escort will be here in a moment." She smiled, trying to keep Luna busy by fussing with her dress some more.

Just when Margie was starting to look like she was running out of things to fuss over, there came a knock at the door.

"Your escort has arrived." Margie rushed over, opening the door.

Once again, Lucas stood on the other side, his jacket matching Luna's dress. Someone was sure going out of their way to make sure they looked like a pair.

Luna rolled her eyes and walked towards him, tucking her arm into his as Margie watched, her eyes twinkling with excitement.

"Dinner, Lady Blackwater?" Lucas asked formally as Margie watched.

Luna nodded, listening as the door closed behind her.

"I have questions." Luna hissed once Margie was out of earshot.

"This is Ezzie's doing, isn't it?" Lucas sighed, "What kind of trouble did you get into."

"None." Luna was surprised, "She was really nice actually. I had a lot of fun. And I learned a lot about Eranox." Luna insisted. "But now I have questions."

"It's a much less formal dinner tonight, just the family." Lucas informed her, "You may have time for some questions. If not, the council is meeting this evening." He added.

"Will you be there?"

"As long as you are here, they are allowing it." He frowned.

Lucas led Luna past the doors to the great hall to a different dining room. There was only one table, and it looked much more cozy and more relaxed.

There were three people waiting in the room, the King, Ezzie and a very pregnant lady that Luna had never seen before sitting at the table.

"Lady Blackwater." The woman nodded to her from her seat, "It is a pleasure to finally meet you."

"This is my mom, Queen Annalise." Lucas introduced her. "She has been on bed rest." He explained.

"It is nice to meet you." Luna slid in at the table.

"Here's to a nice change." The King raised a glass. "No servants this evening, just a nice family meal with our guest." He took a drink.

"No servants?" Luna asked, glancing at Ezzie.

"No." Lucas answered.

"Just some nice time with the family." Queen Annalise added with a smile.

The food was all laid out in the center of the table, and the room was warm. Luna felt more at home, finally able to be herself without pretending to be the Lady Blackwater that Eranox expected of her.

"Could you pass the buns?" Ezzie asked, already filling her plate.

"Well, what do you think of Eranox?" The King asked, handing the basket across the table to Ezzie, his eyes on Luna.

"It's nice." She scooped herself something that looked like mashed potatoes. "But what's past the Gateway?" Ezzie had already told her, but she wanted to hear from the King, see how he reacted.

"Not much these days." He answered, "I suppose we owe you the truth." He added.

Ezzie leaned forward, ready to hear the rest.

"Some of the Northern Villages still send Gwin, they are walled off and surviving. But yes, Luna, the curse is beyond the Gateway."

"So when the city of Eranox is cured, how will we help them?" She wondered. If Eranox was as big as Earth, curing the cursed could take an entire lifetime.

"First the city." The King smiled, "One step at a time." He began to eat, ending their conversation.

Luna ate with Lucas' family, a welcome change to all the formal meals that she had attended in the castle, the food was delicious, similar to her favorites back home on Earth.

"Oh, this is good." Ezzie turned over a spoonful of the thing that Luna thought was mashed potatoes.

"It's an Earth food." Lucas explained, revealing the secret.

"This is all Earth food?" Luna asked, realizing why it was all so familiar.

"As close to as I could get the cook to make it." Lucas nodded. "I thought you'd be missing home by now."

"That was very kind of you Lucas." His mom chimed in, "and Lady Blackwater, the food from Earth is indeed delicious."

"That means a lot coming from Mom." Ezzie added, "She's been sick off of almost every food here."

"It seems this baby enjoys Earth food." Queen Annalise patted her round stomach, "Could be a sign of a traveler." She smiled at Ezzie.

"You're going to let the baby go to Earth before me…" Ezzie pouted.

"I told you I would take you to Earth." Luna reminded Ezzie, "Once it's safe again. Wait until you see the shopping there…" She laughed, imaging Ezzie trying to make sense of the stores on Earth.

"You can't say no to Lady Blackwater." Ezzie smirked at her mom.

"It seems that I cannot." She agreed, "That sounds like a lovely plan."

"Really?" Ezzie looked shocked, "You'd let me?"

"Once the curse is lifted, I don't see why not." The King chimed in.

"You have no idea what you've just gotten yourself into." Lucas muttered, shaking his head.

The door swung open, and suddenly the room went quiet, any cheerful thoughts of traveling to far-away lands were dashed as a Knight entered the room, his eyes wide with wonder.

"My King." He bowed, seeming embarrassed at interrupting their family meal, "I must ask that you come with me." He glanced at Ezzie and Queen Annalise, trying not to alarm them with more details.

"It seems I must excuse myself." The King rose from the table swiftly, as he passed he leaned towards Lucas, "I will send for you two shortly." He whispered, following the Knight out the door.

"Is there Earth dessert?" Ezzie asked, trying to keep the conversation going.

"I should probably be getting back to my room." Her mom answered softly. "Would you ask Dina to help me?" She turned to Ezzie.

"Yes mom." Ezzie rose slowly, she looked disappointed.

"And then go to the kitchens," Lucas suggested, "I asked them to make an Earth dessert called ice cream. You'll love it." Lucas smiled.

"Really?" Ezzie smiled as she rushed from the room.

"You've never had ice cream?" Luna was surprised.

"Not until Earth." Lucas admitted, "Cold things aren't customary in Eranox." He added.

A moment later a servant arrived, wheeling Lucas' mother out of the room. "It was lovely to meet you Lady Blackwater." She tipped her head, "I hope we can speak again soon."

Luna nodded, watching as she was wheeled out back to her room.

"Your mom seems very nice." Luna observed once it was just her and Lucas in the dining room.

"Thanks." Lucas rose from his seat, "She's normally... a little more mobile..." Lucas chuckled, "We should get going, the council will be sending for us shortly."

"What was the rush about?" Luna wondered.

"I expect something happened with the cat." Lucas answered thoughtfully.

"You think it didn't work?" She worried.

"I couldn't tell." He shook his head, "It was hard to read the Knight."

Lucas opened the door and another Knight was standing there, poised to knock. "The King is requesting your presence." He said after a moment, caught off guard by their appearance.

"Thank you, we are on our way." Lucas tipped his head, following the Knight down the hall towards the council chambers.

Luna followed behind, nervous about what they were about to discover. Had the cat been healed, or had she made things worse. There was no way of telling, the guard was so calm and poised, if he had seen something, she couldn't tell.

The Knight held the door for them as they entered the room. The whole council was out of their seats, crowded around the cage in the corner.

Madam Hawthorn turned, seeing them.

"They have arrived." She announced to the others.

The council dispersed, not returning to their seats, but standing to face Luna and Lucas in a semi-circle, blocking the cage.

"Step forward Lady Blackwater." The King requested, waving his arm to his side.

Luna walked forward, terrified of what she was about to see when she finally reached the cage.

She was two steps in when she heard a meow. A simple meow, not garbled and sinister like the sounds from the Gateway. She walked faster, her heart fluttering with excitement.

"It worked." She breathed, staring past the King at the docile cat resting in the cage. It had been given a bowl of milk and was purring as it licked its paws.

"It worked." The King answered, his smile growing.

"And now that we have passed the first test…" Sir Hawthorn stepped closer, a vial in his hand, "It is time to continue." He sounded stoic, his voice flat and even.

"Continue?" Luna knew what the next step was, she wasn't sure that she was ready to face it yet. "Is he here?" She looked around the room for another cage.

"No." Sir Hawthorn answered, shaking his head. "The Knights were not able to procure him."

"They aren't planning on going back into the Gateway at night, are they?" Luna turned to the King, it was a dangerous idea.

"He wasn't able to be found during the day." The King spoke to Lune, "There might be a way to lure him out though…" His voice had taken on a strange pitch that Luna didn't like.

"What are you talking about?" Lucas cut in, stepping in front of Luna to protect her.

"He came to his daughter, he aided her in the Gateway." Sir Hawthorn seemed to be justifying something.

"You can't send her out there." Lucas stomped his foot, raising his voice. "She is the *last* High Wizard… we can't lose her." He reminded them.

"We need another High Wizard," Madam Hawthorn cut in, her voice kind and stern, "and there is only one way to get to him…"

Clearly they had already discussed their plan while Lucas and Luna had still been in the dining room waiting to be summoned, they had made up their minds about how they were going to procure Alec from the Gateway.

"What *is* the plan?" Luna asked, no one had bothered to come straight out with it yet and it was making her dizzy trying to follow the discussion.

The room went silent and the council turned to face her.

"They want to use you as bait." Lucas answered before they could.

"How?" She turned to the council, watching their guilty faces.

"We just need you to call to him." Madam Hawthorn made it sound easy.

"There would be Knights with you, they would keep you safe." Sir Hawthorn added as though that made the difference.

"What about all of the others? The rest of the cursed ones?" Luna asked.

There were cursed in Eranox, and more cursed in the Gateway, how were they supposed to track down just one man without the others coming for them.

"It should be very safe." Sir Hawthorn didn't sound as sure as he had clearly wanted to.

"It's not a good idea." Lucas interjected before they could continue, "You are putting her in danger." He added. "Wouldn't it be better to find someone else, someone different to cure? Can't you find Sir Alec later?"

"The cursed are non-responsive in daylight." Madam Hawthorn reminded Lucas, shooting him a stern look for speaking his mind, "and the Gateway is a very large place. We don't have weeks to find him… Eranox only has days…"

"Days?" Luna asked, surprised, "Is it spreading that fast?" She turned to the King, waiting for an answer.

"I'm afraid so." He answered, "At the rate it is spreading, you couldn't possibly cure enough to stop it from taking over, we *need* a second High Wizard." He looked uncomfortable at the idea of sending Luna out into the Gateway, but it was clear that there was no other way.

Luna looked at the cage, the cat inside seemed content, it had been cured. She was capable of doing what they needed, of lifting the curse. But her mom had been right, they needed to put her in danger to save the rest of Eranox, they needed two High Wizards, one wasn't enough.

"Okay." Luna nodded.

"What?" Lucas turned, "You can't really be considering… I promised that I would keep you safe…"

"We need another High Wizard, to get ahead of the curse." Luna explained her reasons, "I have to go get him, he will come if I ask."

"You really think he is just going to answer you if you call for him? That nothing else out there will come running?"

Lucas shook his head, "This isn't a good idea, it isn't going to end well…" He stared at his father, defiance in his eyes.

"He will come." Luna was sure of it, "He came before when I needed him, I *know* he will come." She didn't know how she knew, she just did.

"But what about the other creatures, the others in the Gateway who are cursed?" Lucas crossed his arms, "They will hear you." He shook his head, "It won't work."

"There will be Knights," Luna looked at the council for reassurance, Sir Hawthorn nodded enthusiastically.

"Ten of them." He noted proudly.

"Then I am going with you." Lucas stepped forward, daring his father to say no to him.

"Are you sure?" The King asked, he had a look in his eye. Things weren't going as he had planned, he didn't want his son out in the Gateway after dark, but he couldn't say no, not if he was sending Luna.

"I am where Luna is." Lucas answered defiantly.

"The Prince has made his choice." Sir Hawthorn looked less than upset that Lucas was choosing to go on a suicide mission into the Gateway.

His Father nodded, "Then so be it." He sounded scared.

"The Knights are prepared to go." Sir Hawthorn interrupted the silence that followed, "We shouldn't waste time." He added, trying to rush things along.

"I'll need to change before I can leave." Luna added, she wasn't about to go running into the Gateway in a fancy dress and heels. She needed to be able to move, she needed to be prepared to run.

"Take her to her quarters." Madam Hawthorn instructed Lucas, "And return quickly." She added pointedly.

Lucas nodded, taking Luna's hand and pulling her towards the chamber doors and out into the hall.

"You must be crazy to agree to that." He walked quickly down the hall towards her room, "And your mom is going to kill me…" He added.

"She doesn't have to know." Luna reminded him, "As long as it all goes well, she never will." Luna promised, though she was starting to feel the fear that was radiating from Lucas.

They reached her room and Luna slipped inside, Margie seemed surprised to see Luna in such a rush. "Just my jeans and a t-shirt." Luna asked as Margie helped her escape the dress she had worn to dinner, "I'll need my Earth shoes too." She added, realizing that she was still wearing heels.

"You aren't leaving, are you?" Margie sounded worried, she hovered between Luna and the door for a moment as though she was going to try to stop her.

"No Margie, I will be back, hopefully tonight…" She promised, zipping up her jeans and reaching for her sneakers by the door. "The Knights will be with me." She added, sure that it would appease Margie's worries to know that her charge was being guarded, and *not* trying to escape again.

In an instant she was back in the hall, but Lucas was nowhere to be found. She did her best to find her way towards the front doors of the castle where she was sure the Knights were waiting. It was getting easier to navigate through the hallways as she became more familiar with the castle, soon she found her way to the doors.

"Where is Prince Lucas, Lady Blackwater?" The Knight at the front looked down the hall, searching for him.

"I'm not sure." Luna answered, "But we should get going."

Luna glanced over her shoulder, she felt bad for leaving Lucas behind, but it was for his own good. It was bad enough that they had asked her to go into the Gateway, but she couldn't risk Eranox losing a High Wizard and a Prince in the same night.

The Knights drew their weapons, prepared to open the doors to the horrors of the night when Luna heard footsteps racing up the hall behind her.

"You're not going anywhere without me." Lucas ran towards her, wearing his own Earth clothes for easier mobility.

The Knights nodded, and pulled open the doors.

Luna could hear it the moment the dark air entered the castle, the screams of the cursed roaming the streets of Eranox.

They rushed out of the door, listening as the castle was locked behind them.

There were more Knights waiting outside next to a large cage and surprisingly, Sir Hawthorn was there with them.

Sir Hawthorn stepped forward, looking like he was in a hurry to get back into the castle, "This is for you." He held out a strange circle, "It will block your father's magic if you place it on his neck, making transport easier." He added.

Luna reached for the item, but Lucas took it from Sir Hawthorn's hand first, "I will carry it, we might need your magic…" He said to Luna.

"Probably best." Sir Hawthorn nodded in agreement, "Best of luck." He added, walking towards the front doors to escape the night.

"Ten Knights." Lucas counted, "I hope that's enough."

"We can do this." Luna promised, she hoped that saying it aloud would make it true, there was already a knot in her stomach at the thought of seeing the dark man from her nightmares again.

This time she would be looking for him.

Two of the Knights pulled the cage forward, the others falling in step behind it as it led the way. It looked like something out of a circus, a tall brass cage on wheels, and she knew what it was for.

They were going to cage the cursed one.

Quietly they escaped the castle grounds, walking the streets of Eranox in silence, the rattle of the cage leading the way.

FOURTEEN

Eranox appeared to be empty, the inhabitants had locked themselves inside before the night time curfew had fallen, keeping themselves safe from the cursed that roamed the streets inside of the city. The cheerful storefronts that Luna had seen in the daylight had been expertly boarded up, preventing the creatures of the night from breaking through to the stores and homes beyond.

Luna could hear them, the cursed, as they wandered through the streets howling and screaming as they searched for their next victims. The Knights seemed on edge as they guarded Luna and Lucas on their way towards the Gateway, each squeak of the wheels on the cage caused them to jump. They walked with their swords drawn, ready for an attack as they scoured the streets for the creatures while they moved.

The dark howls echoed through the streets, some were far off in the distance, others eerily close. Though Luna hadn't spotted anything out of the usual as she walked the streets, her eyes scanned every dark corner for something watching her.

In the distance someone screamed, and Luna could hear the scrambling as the creatures honed in on their target. Though she tried not to think about it, she knew what had happened, there was another cursed being born.

"Stay close." Lucas whispered, walking so close to Luna's side that she was sure she was going to trip over him.

"I will." She answered, keeping pace with the Knights and the cage.

By some luck, more likely some bad luck for someone else in Eranox, they finally managed to get to the doors of the Gateway without encountering any of the dangers that roamed within the walls.

And then the caravan stopped. The Knights stepped away from the cage and stared up at the doors, their faced drawn with worry.

"The door doesn't open at night..." Lucas stared ahead as the Knights began to move again, assembling something to the side of the entrance to the Gateway.

"Then how are they planning on getting in?" Luna asked, edging towards the Knights, wary of being left alone in the streets while they were busy with whatever it was that they were doing.

As soon as they got closer it became apparent. "Looks like we're using a ladder." Luna observed, watching as the Knights tipped up the creation and secured it to the wall with care.

"You have got to be kidding me." Lucas sighed, walking forward to join her as she watched them work.

The Knights finished securing the ladder to the wall and the head Knight turned back, "Two Knights will remain." He informed them, "To guard the ladder and protect the cage." He added to clarify.

"Do you think a Ladder will be safe?" Lucas asked, watching the top of the wall warily.

"It will have to do." The head Knight shook his head as though he agreed with Lucas' assessment. "This is it."

Luna nodded, her heart beating loudly in her chest. She was nervous, but it was too late to turn back, she was going to have to go into the Gateway again.

"We will enter the Gateway first Lady Blackwater, to ensure that it is safe before you and Prince Lucas join us." He added, turning as the first Knight slowly began to climb the ladder.

Luna didn't envy him.

He looked hesitant, clearly he had drawn the short straw and been given the task of being the first to cross over the wall. When he reached the top of the wall he paused, glancing into the abyss on the other side carefully before he tossed a second rope ladder over and began his descent into the Gateway and out of sight.

Luna listened as the Knights clamored over the wall after him. The Gateway was surprisingly quiet, quieter than she had ever heard it. Even Eranox had gone silent, like the calm before a storm. She looked at Lucas, "Do you think they are waiting?" She whispered, afraid that the creatures had already sensed them and were just waiting for the opportunity to strike.

"They are smarter than the Knights will ever know, it's very possible." Lucas answered thoughtfully, "Just promise you will stay near me once we are in there…" He asked her pleadingly, he really seemed to be taking his promise to Luna's mom seriously.

"I will." Luna agreed, she didn't plan on being alone in the Gateway at night again, and at least she knew Lucas could find his way around.

Her heart fluttered as the last Knight tipped over the top of the wall disappearing, "Here we go." She whispered, preparing herself as she reached for the ladder.

Luna pulled herself up to the top of the wall, one rung at a time. When she reached the top she paused for a moment to stare over the Gateway, wondering where her father could be in the massive maze. She couldn't see anything inside of the twisting walls but darkness.

Lucas was right behind her, stuck on the ladder while he waited for her to move, "Are you going down?" He asked, still waiting for Luna to make up her mind as she teetered at the top of the wall staring off into the Gateway.

Luna nodded and turned herself to grab on to the other side of the ladder as she began to lower herself into the darkness waiting below her.

The Knights were waiting for her in the dark, the quiet ping of their armor giving them away as they fidgeted. They were waiting for Lady Blackwater to call the cursed and bring forth the lost High Wizard like it was a simple task.

Luna still wasn't sure how they expected her to accomplish the task without alerting every creature in the Gateway and drawing them to the entrance where they were waiting. She knew that if she called for him, the dark creature that was her father, that the others would hear her; but she would try her best to call only him, for fear of her own life and the others that were with her.

As her feet finally found the ground she stepped away from the ladder, turning towards the sounds of the waiting Knights. She closed her eyes, wondering if she could find her father with her mind, in the same way that she had found the curse within the caged cat. The darkness consumed her, she tried to concentrate, finding the Knights with her mind, their energies appearing brightly in her head, and then she ventured farther, out through the winding pathways, lost in the darkness, and she called to him.

Find me, she thought with her mind focused on the Gateway, *find me now,* she urged, hoping that he was the only creature hearing her thoughts.

Lucas landed behind her quietly and she opened her eyes, not sure if her call had worked. He stepped up beside her as the Knights turned to watch, their armor catching patches of light from the moons overhead as the clouds rolled away.

"Are you ready Lady Blackwater?" The lead Knight asked, slowly he drew his sword from his side the blade scraping against his chest.

"Yes." Luna answered, but it sounded like a lie the moment it escaped her lips.

"Are you sure?" Lucas mumbled, keeping his voice low.

"We can do this." Luna righted her shoulders, too proud to turn back.

The head Knight stepped to Luna's side, "Lead the way, we will protect you." He instructed.

In a moment the Knights had taken their ranks, two at Luna's side and six more behind her for protection. Lucas was directly behind her, there was no room at her side for him. She felt safer knowing that someone she trusted had her back.

Luna took one step forward and closed her eyes for a moment, wondering if her father had answered her call, curious if she could find him in the Gateway and make her task easier. But all she could feel was her heart beating in her chest, the ringing in her ears, her breaths short and raspy. She was terrified about what she was going to find, or more likely, what was going to find her hidden between those high walls in the dark.

She was going to have to find another way to locate their target, behind her the Knights shuffled their feet impatiently, waiting for her to make up her mind, clearly they wanted to get the task done and over with so they could leave the Gateway behind them for the safety of their own homes.

Finally Luna decided that she would lead the small army away from the entrance before she called to her father, that way if the other creatures found them first they would still have a safe escape back into Eranox.

She didn't waste time explaining herself, slowly she began to walk through the Gateway. The clinking of the Knights' armor surrounded her and made it difficult to hear much of the noise out in the rest of the dark space ahead of her, so she kept her pace slow and steady while she strained to hear farther.

Each turn she had to pause and wait for the Knights to stop moving so she could hear if there was danger ahead. It was a slow process, she only hoped that her caution would keep them safe and they would all survive.

The Gateway remained quiet, eerily so, she couldn't hear the creatures howling, nor the scraping of their claws as they traveled along the dark stone paths. It was unsettling, knowing that they were out there and not knowing where.

Once she thought she was far enough from the door and the ladder to Eranox, Luna stopped walking.

"Here." She turned back, whispering to the Knights that they were not going any farther into the maze. "I will call him from here."

The Knights circled around her wordlessly, ready for her to make the call that would bring Sir Alec out from the darkness.

"Before you do this… are you absolutely sure?" Lucas asked, standing at her side, protected by the circle of Knights.

Luna could see the fear in his eyes.

"I have to." Luna shook her head, trying to stay calm, "There is no point in turning back now, if I don't… this is it for your world." She added quietly.

"Thank you." Lucas nodded, understanding that she was going to go through with it.

They were already in the Gateway, the Knights had already taken every precaution, and they had already taken the risk of going in with her. If Luna gave up now there was no second chance. Either she called for her father, or Eranox had to hope for a miracle as the curse consumed them all.

Luna listened, trying to focus on the sounds in the Gateway around her, unsure if it really mattered which way she shouted into the night.

"Alec Blackwater?" She called his name, her voice cracking, "Dad?" She shouted into the wind, her words echoing through the path growing quieter until they faded into nothing.

It happened almost instantaneously, the howls inside of the Gateway grew louder, answering her as the creatures honed in on the voice in the maze that was calling to them.

"Get ready." Lucas hissed, warning the Knights as he prepared himself for the inevitable.

The Knights shifted, readying themselves for what was coming. A few seconds later the first creature appeared, ripping around the corner towards them. There was nowhere to hide, Luna was going to have to face the creature, the Knights swords wouldn't do anything against the sharp claws and gaping jaw that was approaching. The Knights braced themselves, swords drawn, but they wouldn't stop anything. Luna let her instincts take over, remembering the fire that Lucas had taught her how to create.

She shot her hands forward between the Knights, remembering a moment too late that the creatures in the Gateway were still human beneath their curse. A great ball of fire careened forward through the path, knocking the creature aside, but surprisingly it seemed unharmed otherwise.

The creatures stopped in its tracks, staring at Luna quietly. Though it didn't dare edge any closer than it already was, it still didn't back away. Another creature appeared at its side and Luna prepared to fire again, but the second creature stopped too, sniffing the air with curiosity.

Behind her, Luna could hear the other Knights scrambling as they tried to fend off the creatures that had come from the other side of the path.

She tilted her head, trying to watch what was happening behind her without losing sight of the two creatures that had paused on the path in front of her.

"Retreat." One of the Knights shouted.

"Fall back." Another commanded.

Slowly the circle of Knights pressed in around her and began backing up the path, edging towards the door to Eranox and the waiting ladder.

The creatures moved with them, making Luna's plan for a safe escape nonexistent. They weren't getting out of the Gateway without a fight, and they still had seen no sign of their actual target.

As they backed around the final corner Luna glanced towards the exit. A lone Knight was perched atop the wall, the rope ladder recoiled and waiting in his hands. He wasn't giving the creatures a chance to escape the Gateway, but he wasn't letting them out either.

"Back up." A Knight shouted.

Luna pressed her hand between their ranks and blasted a ball of fire again, giving the Knights at the front enough space to make it back around the corner as the creatures backed off momentarily.

"We're trapped." Lucas screamed, staring up at the Knight on top of the wall, his eyes wide.

They were backed up into the doors, the doors that wouldn't open at night, and the creatures had them cornered.

The plan had derailed, it had gone horribly wrong and now they were trapped in the Gateway, surrounded by the cursed creatures with no way out.

Luna was running out of energy, she wasn't sure that she could even create another fireball if she tried. Not that it would matter, the fire didn't seem to hurt the cursed creatures roaming through the Gateway. And night had only just fallen, there was no way that they could fend off the creatures until dawn.

The Knights had pulled out their shields, creating a wall as they backed in to surround Lucas and Luna, protecting them from the beasts on the other side, but it wouldn't last for long.

The ting of claws scraping against the shields rung out into the night. At the top of the wall the Knight with the ladder was watching, the rope coiled in his hands. He stared down at them with horror, unable to help them, unwilling to let the ladder down while the creatures were so near and so many.

"Do something, let us out." Lucas shouted up to him, his voice straining with terror.

He shook his head, watching beyond the wall of shields, whatever it was that he could see had struck fear in him, he wasn't letting the ladder down.

"He's here." The Knight shouted down to them, his eyes wide with disbelief.

A second later the scratching stopped. Luna could still hear the creatures, their deep gravely breaths echoing in the chamber surrounding them.

But they had stopped attacking, and then she felt it.

Like a tugging on the back of her mind, Luna closed her eyes, feeling through the dark for it.

I am here, his voice was dark and wispy, like it had been caught on the wind and carried into her head.

"It's him." Luna confirmed as she opened her eyes, watching the shields, knowing that he was there on the other side, he was the thing that the Knight on the wall had seen.

One of the Knights lowered his shield so they could see to the other side.

There he stood, like a darkness that had swallowed all of the shadows, so dark that the light from the moons overhead were lost in him; Alec Blackwater, the cursed High Wizard, the one they had come for.

He stood at the center of the creatures, somehow commanding them as though he was their master. They knelt at his dark silhouette, unmoving, obeying his demands, and Luna was sure that he had control over them.

They were still in danger.

"Let him in." Luna commanded to the Knights.

They stepped aside, allowing the dark shape to step into their ranks, reinstating their wall of shields the moment that he was inside so they could keep the creatures from joining him.

He stepped towards Luna, stopping as he neared.

You called me, she heard his voice, though the dark shape before her didn't flinch.

Luna stared at him, the terror from her nightmares returning, standing as real as she was, right in front of her.

"You heard me?" She asked.

He didn't answer.

Lucas crept around the circle, keeping at the Knights backs as he made his way behind Alec.

"I called you, and you came…" Luna stared at him, hoping her distraction would last.

Lucas turned, fastening the collar around the dark neck of their visitor.

If he was alarmed, he didn't show it. In fact, he didn't move at all. He just stood there, staring at Luna.

And then he collapsed.

FIFTEEN

The moment Alec Blackwater collapsed to the stone floor, the creatures resumed their attack on the circle of Knights. It was as though they sensed that Alec had fallen, like they were trying to get to him.

In an instant the Knights were fending them off again with their shields, trying to keep them at bay while the Knight atop the wall reconsidered allowing them an escape now that they had the lost High Wizard captured with them. He was weighing his options, they had accomplished their task, but the danger was still present and the risk was high.

"Let us out." Lucas shouted up at him, waving his hands.

Finally the rope ladder was tossed down, and without hesitation, Lucas and Luna began to climb, leaving the Gateway behind them.

Luna hurried over the top, clamoring to get down the other side. When she finally reached the bottom, she dropped to her knees. Her heart was racing, using the fire had taken most of her energy and she was reeling at the close calls that they had narrowly escaped with the cursed creatures, though she knew that they were not safe yet.

They wouldn't be safe until they were back at the castle, until the doors were closed and locked to the terrors of the night behind them. They weren't done yet.

She could still hear the creatures on the other side of the wall, growling and clawing at the Knights and their shields as they tried to get through to attack. The Knights were shouting, backing towards the ladder as they took the risk of making a hasty escape from the Gateway.

"Now what do we do?" Luna turned, watching the wall as Lucas landed on the ground.

"I don't know, no one told us what would happen if we found him…" He breathed, looking for the other Knight to find out what was about to happen.

"Ready the cage." The Knight atop the wall shouted down.

Lucas paused, watching as the Knight on the ground produced a key, reaching for a lock on the cage, a moment later the cage was open and the Knight stood waiting with the brass barred door in his hand.

"What are they doing?" Luna asked, pointing to the top of the wall where a second Knight had appeared.

"They're pulling him up." Lucas observed, watching with Luna as the two Knights at the top of the wall strained to haul something up to the top with ropes, a moment later the prone form of the dark man appeared. They had their captive tied up, carefully they shifted him over to the other side of the wall and began to lower him down into Eranox where the cage was waiting to contain him.

Quietly he landed at the bottom of the ladder, Luna stared at the lifeless shape of the dark creature that had at one time been a High Wizard, her father.

"Should we help him?" She asked.

"No Luna, they have it." Lucas answered as the two Knights quickly scrambled down the ladder, retrieving him from the ground and carrying him to the waiting cage.

He didn't put up a fight, he didn't even flinch as they locked his limp body in the ornate cage, he seemed so small and helpless that for a moment Luna felt bad for him.

Luna kept staring at the cage while the rest of the Knights returned from the Gateway and began to disassemble the ladder, their task complete.

"Luna?" Lucas prodded her shoulder breaking her stare a few minutes later, "It's time to go."

Luna looked around at the team, ready to make the trip back to the castle, they were short a Knight.

"There are only nine Knights." She turned, her eyes wide as she counted again. "There are only nine…" She didn't understand why she couldn't find the tenth.

They had already removed the ladders from the great wall, the cart had been hoisted up and was ready to begin moving. She turned to Lucas, "There are only nine, there were ten before." She repeated, it was like no one was hearing her.

"Kevin was bitten." A Knight beside Luna answered bitterly, "He remains behind for the safety of the city." He carried two shields and a sense of defeat.

"What?" Luna spun around, without thinking she was already racing back towards the doors to the Gateway. They had left someone behind, it wasn't fair, they couldn't leave someone behind, not in the Gateway.

"He has to stay." A Knight held Luna's shoulder, stopping her from reaching the doors.

"Can't we put him in the cage, can't we save him?" She asked.

A look flashed across the Knights face, surprise, he hadn't been expecting Luna to care, the loss of one of the Knights was clearly a sacrifice that they had been willing to make.

"It's too late now Lady Blackwater, they have taken him." He shook his head, his heart broken, "We cannot risk going back in there… we must return to the castle." He trailed off.

"But we got the High Wizard." Lucas cut in, turning Luna gently away from the doors to the Gateway and the Knights so he could talk to her, "We got your father, and that

Knight can still be saved, all of Eranox can still be saved." He added, trying to cheer Luna up.

"…Eranox still has a chance… He can still be saved…" Luna nodded, though it meant that there was one more of the cursed in the Gateway who would need saving, the pros outweighed the cons.

"Exactly." Lucas smiled, watching Luna's face carefully. "We did it."

Luna smiled, at least the worst was now behind them.

"Stay close." The head Knight warned as the cart began to roll forward and the entourage of Knights fell into place, guiding them back towards the castle.

Luna and Lucas fell into step with the Knights behind the cart as it rolled through the city, they weren't done yet.

From between the passing buildings Luna could feel them, the cursed in the streets of Eranox. Though they weren't as bold as those in the Gateway, she knew that they were there. They snarled, barring their teeth as the caravan passed, not daring to step out of the shadows, but watching.

Lucas seemed nervous, he walked so close to Luna that she was sure he was going to step on her feet, his eyes darting towards the buildings as he watched the streets.

"Why aren't they attacking?" Luna whispered as they passed another alley, a creature hissing at them from the darkness.

"I don't know…" Lucas looked shaken, "It has to be something about him, he seemed to have some control over the others in the Gateway…" Lucas stared ahead at the cage, though Alec Blackwater was still unconscious, unmoving at the bottom of the cage, the creatures still seemed hesitant to attack them.

Luna nodded, not sure what to make of Lucas' observation. The creatures in the Gateway had stopped when he had arrived, and then Lucas had placed the collar around his neck and he had collapsed; perhaps they were trying to protect him.

If the cursed had a leader, and they were able to cure him; it was going to make a big difference.

Silence washed back over them as they passed through the dark street, the castle looming ahead of them still off in the distance.

More than once Luna caught a glimpse of someone watching them through a window as they passed. The curious onlookers risking letting the cursed see them so they could catch a glimpse of the gilded cage as it passed them by.

"Do they know?" Luna wondered aloud as she caught the stare of another watcher from a window above a boarded storefront.

"They all know." Lucas nodded, "By morning the whole city will know that Alec Blackwater is back at the castle." He added.

"I guess there are no secrets here… it's kind of like River Falls.." Luna murmured, realizing that Eranox would be expecting her to save the High Wizard before dawn. Word would spread fast, and if she wasn't able to do it they would lose their only hopes for survival.

She wasn't sure that she had the energy left, after her trip into the Gateway she was drained. It was a lot of pressure on her, expecting her to cure Alec that same night.

"Are you okay?" Lucas was staring at her, they were nearing the castle gates and she had started walking slower to give herself more time; he had noticed.

Luna nodded, she didn't have the energy to explain to Lucas how she was feeling about the whole ordeal. How could she explain to him how much the weight of Eranox was pulling down on her? How could he possibly understand? She couldn't let him know, he had promised to protect her, she didn't want to make him choose between her and his home world.

Ahead the cage rumbled through the gates, the dark creature from her nightmare was still curled up in a ball on the floor of the cage, he hadn't moved once. It was hard to imagine that he was just a normal person, her father, the once High Wizard of Eranox.

It was hard to imagine just how far he had fallen.

Sir Hawthorn was waiting for them at the front doors with his own entourage of Knights. They must have been watching from a tower, Luna couldn't imagine that he would have waited outside at night and put himself in danger any longer than he needed to.

"Come now." He called to Lucas and Luna as the cage was pulled past him to another door of the castle.

"Where are they going?" Luna asked Lucas quietly, watching as the cage rolled out of sight.

"They have to take it around back, probably through the dungeons." He shrugged, hopping up the front steps to meet Sir Hawthorn, eager to put their harrowing adventure behind him.

Luna followed them inside.

The castle was warm, as she stepped inside Luna felt the chill of the night leaving her at the door. But her desire to stall for time remained.

"Come now Lady Blackwater, the council is waiting." Sir Hawthorn glanced over his shoulder as he walked away into the castle, hurried to get the meeting started.

"Come on Luna." Lucas hissed, rushing to catch up.

Luna followed, taking her time as she turned through the castle halls towards the council chambers. She wouldn't have time to change and make herself suitable for their meeting, though she didn't really care. She was more comfortable in her Earth clothes, and they were asking a lot of her, her wardrobe should be the last thing they were worrying about.

Lucas was waiting for her outside of the council room doors as she turned the last corner.

"Aren't you coming in?" Luna asked, watching as he shuffled his feet, staying outside of the room.

"I've been asked to stay outside," He glanced into the room sheepishly, the council was waiting. "But I will be right here if you need me." He added apologetically.

"Really?" Luna was surprised that they had changed their minds, what was so different about this meeting that Lucas wasn't allowed inside with her? Was it because he had defied his father and gone with her into the Gateway?

"I'll be right here, I promise." Lucas stared at her, "They need you inside." He added in a whisper when she didn't keep walking.

Luna nodded and looked into the room, stepping over the threshold as Lucas closed the door behind her. She walked slowly towards the council, they were staring at her.

"Lady Blackwater." The King turned to address her, tipping his head in greeting. "We are pleased to see that you have returned unharmed."

Behind him the cage had entered the room like a spectacle for their amusement. She stared past the King at the creature waiting for her in the gilded cage, wondering what had become of him.

"Lady Blackwater?" The King was staring at her, "Are you alright?" He asked as though he had been talking to her for a while and she hadn't noticed.

Luna stared at the cage for a moment longer. Inside Alec Blackwater, or the curse that had consumed him, was beginning to regain consciousness. The collar had been removed and her nightmares were flashing vividly in her mind.

Finally she looked away, "Yes." She answered the King slowly, her eyes turning to him.

"We know it is late, and you have already been through an ordeal this night…" The King stepped towards her, "Do you think you could try?"

It was the very last thing that Luna wanted to do, dealing with the creature that had once been her father. But as she looked around the room at the staring council members she knew that she had to at least try, she wasn't sure that they would even let her leave unless she did.

Success could mean that Eranox was saved, and judging by how fast words spread in the Kingdom, it would buy them enough time to get the cure started.

Luna nodded, "Okay." She agreed reluctantly, "Do you have the vial?"

Sir Hawthorn stepped forward, handing her a container. It was much larger than the vial she had used to cure the cat, but a human would probably take more potion to separate the curse.

Luna took the bottle and glanced back at the cage, "How do I get up there?" She asked staring at the top of it.

A ladder was already being brought into the room by two Knights, they rested it against the cage.

Luna nodded, not waiting for their prompt. The sooner she tried, the sooner it would all be done with.

Carefully she climbed the ladder to the top of the cage, wary of the stirring form still resting inside. She uncorked the bottle and poured it atop the shape before he could squirm out of the way or reach his dark hand through the cage to knock over her ladder. And then, as quickly as possible, she climbed back down and got away from the ladder.

Inside the cage the dark creature that had consumed Alec Blackwater had begun to howl, his deep throaty call echoing in the small chamber.

It was terrifying.

"You'll have to work quickly." The King stepped back from the cage, leaving Luna there on her own to face the cursed man inside. "He's calling the others." He warned.

Luna had nearly forgotten that there were still cursed inside of Eranox. She didn't want to find out what kinds of creatures her father was calling, his screams echoed around her.

"Okay." She breathed, steeling herself as she reached her hand out towards him.

The creature inside the cage stopped, and turned towards her, watching her with his dark eyes.

I'm still here. His voice echoed in her head, though the creature continued to howl. Luna stared into his dark eyes, trying to find the spark of him that was still human, it was speaking to her, it was still there. It gave her hope that he could still be saved, though she knew that the curse had had much longer to consume him than the freshly cursed cat that she had already cured.

Luna closed her eyes so she could focus without seeing him in front of her watching. She felt for the curse on him, it was thicker than it had been on the cat, more intertwined with the still-human aspects of him. It had been there longer and twisted through him like a parasite, connected to every part of him. But she could still feel it, like a cold layer that had wrapped itself through him.

The darkness seemed to be more alive, it twisted and wriggled to get away from her as she tried to concentrate. Perhaps it was just that his curse had been there longer, but a part of Luna suspected that it was because night had fallen and the curse was active, it had more energy to fight back.

In her mind she imagined the curse lifting, twisting from his body into the air and turning to smoke. She didn't want to leave any trace behind so she concentrated harder, pressing her hand into the air in front of her, watching with her mind as the smoke lifted, dissipating in the air above the cage.

She heard the King gasp, but dared not open her eyes for another moment as she made sure that there was no sign of the curse left on the caged man. She dug deeper, reaching into the recesses of his being, drawing out the stubborn dark spots that tried to cling to him and dissolving them into nothing.

Slowly Luna opened her eyes, the world seemed spotted before her. Her head was spinning.

"You did it." The King breathed.

Luna stared at the cage, where there had once been a dark smoky creature there was now a man. His clothes were ragged, and his hair wild, he curled himself into a ball, looking at his hands.

And then he looked up.

His eyes were dark and curious, they reminded Luna of her own. He stared at her for a moment longer, his eyes welling with tears.

"Luna?" He gasped, the word crackling through his dry throat, "Luna…"

A tightness formed in Luna's throat, she was overwhelmed. There before her, still trapped in a cage, was the father she had never known. She didn't even know what to say, she didn't know how he knew her name. Her head was spinning, her knees were weak. It had taken every ounce of energy she had had left to release him from the curse.

The world twisted around her as she fell to the ground.

SIXTEEN

Something brushed against Luna's face, she turned her head, her eyes fluttering open. There was a canopy over her head, and warm blankets wrapped up to her neck.

She was back in her own room, or at least her room in Eranox.

"You're awake Miss." She felt a bump as Margie sat at the end of the bed staring at her.

Luna sat up, leaning against the heavy pillows to look around.

"What happened?" Luna asked quietly.

She didn't remember getting to her room, she didn't remember much at all about the night before. It seemed like a vivid nightmare that she couldn't shake, the Gateway, the dark man, a cage; it was hard to piece together in a way that made any sense.

Margie shook her head, "The council should have known better..." She tisked, looking Luna over, "They worked you far too hard, when you were brought up you were in very bad shape."

"Who brought me up?" Luna asked, she didn't remember getting back to her room, she must have been half asleep.

Margie shook her head, "It took two of them to get you in here, you were unconscious." Margie stared into Luna's eyes, searching for a sign that she was injured.

"I was?"

"You must have fainted." Margie turned away, "It was too much, they worked you too hard."

Margie seemed to be rustling with something in her apron, a moment later she pulled out a small glass container with some sort of lotion in it. "Here, give me your hands." Margie slathered the lotion into her hands and set the jar aside, taking Luna by the palms and massaging the lotion into her skin. "Using powers like that," Margie looked down at Luna's hands, "It takes time, and patience… you are lucky that you appear to be okay." She added.

Luna looked down at her hands, there were scorch marks on her palms.

"What happened?" Luna turned her hands over, looking for more marks.

"You used too much, more than you could handle, it shows." Margie shook her head, "It will take a little longer to heal."

"Did it work?" Luna asked, she remembered the smoky man in the cage, the curse lifting above him and evaporating, and then nothing after.

Margie nodded, "They seemed pleased, I think you managed to impress them." She answered, "How are you feeling?" Margie leaned in closer, feeling Luna's forehead with her wrist like she expected a fever.

"I feel alright, I think…" Luna looked at her hands again, she didn't feel hurt.

"You've slept for nearly half the day." Margie tipped her head knowingly, "You must be hungry…"

"Thirsty…" Luna corrected, realizing how dry her throat was.

Margie nodded, passing Luna a cup of tea that she had rested on the night stand to cool, "This should help, and you should probably eat something too, keep your energy up, it will help you heal faster." She insisted, walking to the door and ringing a bell.

It would seem that there was room service in the castle, and Margie was calling for a meal.

Luna took a sip of the tea, letting it calm her dry throat, "I don't think I'm up for eating right now…" She tried to explain before it was too late.

"Oh don't be silly, you just don't know it yet, but you are starved." Margie gave Luna a knowing look.

"Really Margie, it's okay." Luna finished the tea and tossed the blankets aside, walking towards the wardrobe where her Earth clothes were stored, "I think I would like to go and see the council, I want to know if it worked…"

She tossed her nightdress aside and began to get dressed.

"Here dear, let me help." Margie appeared at her side with a dress and cloak in her arms.

"Thank you." Luna took the cloak and tossed it on over her jeans and t-shirt, at least it was warm.

Margie stared at her with wide eyes, "Are you sure?" She asked politely, trying to hold out the dress for Luna to wear.

"This is much more comfortable." Luna answered, slipping her feet into her sneakers and walking towards the door.

"I should call you an escort." Margie called, racing across the room to try and keep Luna from leaving on her own.

"I think I can find my own way." Luna smiled, stepping out into the hall and leaving Margie behind her.

Luna had only been a few places in the castle, so she was sure that she could find her way back to the council room without getting lost. The winding empty halls of the castle carried her forward, and a few minutes later she found herself faced with a Knight, standing guard outside of the council room doors.

"Lady Blackwater." He tipped his head, surprised to see her.

"I need to see him." Luna pointed to the closed doors, sure that her father was still in there, caged and waiting.

The Knight looked uncomfortable, "I'll have to check Lady Blackwater." He sounded afraid.

Luna nodded, waiting for him to check for her. He knocked on the door, whispering to a Knight on the other side. A moment later he turned back to Luna and nodded, the door swung open for her to enter.

"Thank you." She tipped her head as she passed the Knight, entering the council chambers.

A new cage had been constructed in the middle of the room where the large meeting table had once stood. Though the gilded cage had disappeared, the captive remained.

It was more like a jail cell, inside the man was pacing, the real Alec Blackwater. He looked up when Luna entered the room.

He had been given real clothes, or at least the familiar cloaks of a High Wizard in Eranox, and looked less disheveled than he had the night before when Luna had seen his real face for the first time.

There were two Knights standing guard on either side of the cage, Luna watched them as she approached the bars, a stiff nod from one of them telling her when she had gotten close enough.

The man inside the cell had stopped pacing, he stood in the center of the cage, watching as Luna approached.

"You look so much like your mother." He smiled with a sadness in his eyes. "Did she name you Luna? That was the plan…" He trailed off, looking away from her for a moment as he composed himself.

"She did." Luna watched as he looked back at her.

"Where is she? Is she okay?"

Luna nodded, "She's okay, she is still on Earth." Luna answered, more curious about him than she should have been, "So you're my dad…"

"I suppose I am." He smiled again, though the sadness was still there, "How long…"

"Eighteen years." Luna didn't wait for him to finish the question.

"That long…" He stared off shaking his head, "I can't believe it's been that long…" He admitted quietly.

"Do you remember it?" Luna asked, curious about what it was like being cursed. He seemed to be recovering well enough, she wondered if it would be the same for the others when the curse was finally lifted.

"Some." He looked haunted for a moment, "At times I think I was in control, but that curse…" He shook his head, "It makes you forget things… *do* things… it was hard to control."

"You could control it?" Luna hadn't expected that.

"Only sometimes." He nodded, "Like when I brought you the necklace." He pointed to the stone hanging from her neck.

Luna reached up, feeling the warm red stone in her fingers, "So it *was* you…"

He nodded, "That was the longest that I was ever in control, three days…" He spoke as though it were a well-earned vacation, "and the ring…" He added, looking down at his hands.

"Mom has it now." Luna smiled.

Alec nodded, a small smile played on his lips, washed away a moment later by the sadness.

"How are you feeling?" Luna asked, curing him had knocked her out long enough to waste half the day, she was sure that it would have affected him as well.

"Like I've been frozen for eighteen years." He chuckled, "It's nice to be able to move my arms again." He swung his arms in a circle to prove his point.

"Now what?" Luna asked, "Are they keeping you caged? Are you going to help cure the others?"

What she really wanted to ask was; *can I go home now?*, but she couldn't bring herself to say it, not in front of him.

"I suppose I am in quarantine until they figure that out." He shook his head, "It was impressive what you did." He added with a twinge of pride. "How long have you been training for that?"

"Training?" Luna was afraid to answer, "I didn't…" She admitted sheepishly, "It was the cat, and then you."

"The cat?" Alec nearly laughed.

"Yes, first they had me try it on a cat." She answered.

His face fell, "So you weren't trained?" He sounded disappointed.

Luna shook her head, "I didn't even know about Eranox until last week…"

He sighed, "Then I suppose your mother has moved on…" He spoke quietly, the sadness returning, "I should have expected it, eighteen years is a long time…"

"Moved on?" Luna shook her head, "She thought you were dead, but she never moved on."

"Dead?" Alec looked startled.

"Yeah, I never even knew about you." Luna said quietly, "It's always just been her and me…"

"But she didn't tell you about Eranox?" He began pacing again.

"She wasn't planning on coming back…" Luna whispered, afraid that the Knights would overhead and get her mother in trouble.

"You are a High Wizard, that should have meant something. And to hear that you have never been trained." He stopped and stared at Luna for a moment in silence, "I don't know how you did it…" He trailed off thoughtfully.

"Did it?" Luna stared back at him, trying to read his face.

"How did you lift the curse?" He stepped towards her, still staring, "It shouldn't have been possible…"

"It wasn't easy." Luna admitted, not sure how much of it she was allowed to share, "They came up with the plan on their own."

"And you cured me first." He stopped, considering something, "So I could help..." He trailed off lost in thought.

"They were hoping you could." Luna admitted.

"One at a time..." He turned, pacing again, "It could work..." He mumbled to himself. "It would take time... but it could work..."

Luna watched as he paced in his cell, thinking something through. He made several laps before he finally stopped and turned back to her, looking a little more cheerful, eager even.

"They finally found a way, a way without the others." He smiled, "And once I have survived the night..." He shook his head in disbelief, "We can start to go back to normal..." He breathed.

"Mom's going to be really happy that you're back." Luna smiled, she could imagine the look on her mom's face even then.

"Why isn't she here now?"

Luna considered, "It was too dangerous..." She wasn't sure if that was the right answer. They had only needed Luna, so she hadn't even asked about bringing her mom with her, "I guess it would have been hard on her... especially if we failed." She added.

If she had brought her mom back to Eranox, reunited her with her home and then not been able to save it, it would have been devastating. She couldn't have done that to her, and perhaps that was the reason why her mom hadn't even brought it up. It was much easier for Luna to walk away, she had no history in Eranox, walking away would just be another move for her.

"Yes." He settled himself in, sitting on the floor. "I imagine so."

Luna sat down with him, the safe distance between her and the bars seemed absurd, but she didn't dare edge any closer. "Can you tell me about Eranox?" She asked.

There was a sparkle in her father's eye, like he had been waiting for just that question.

SEVENTEEN

Luna and her father talked well into the afternoon, about everything from life in Eranox before the curse to growing up on Earth. Luna was sure that they wouldn't run out of things to talk about, they had missed *years* of each other's lives.

Though she had imagined meeting her father many times in her life, it had never been like this. She had always thought that he had abandoned them, left without looking back. Finding out that he had been cursed and wandering in a labyrinth with other evils had been strange to her, but talking to him, *really* talking to him, came easier than she had expected.

Luna heard the doors open behind her and knew that her time was up.

"Night must be coming soon Luna." Her father frowned, "You should get going, just in case." He added, the sadness returning to his eyes.

"I know." Luna hesitated, rising to her feet as she stretched out the numbness that had taken her legs over. "I'll come back tomorrow morning." She promised, turning slowly towards the door.

Lucas was standing there, beside him a Knight entered the room carrying a tray, food for her father in his cage. At least they weren't treating him like an animal.

"I'll see you tomorrow." Luna called over her shoulder, not really wanting to leave.

"Tomorrow dear." Her father smiled, pressing his hand against the bars as he said goodbye.

Lucas didn't say a word as Luna followed him into the hall, he seemed different, quieter than usual.

"Do I really have to leave him?" Luna asked Lucas, keeping her voice down, "I *could* eat with him…" She suggested, not wanting to leave Alec in his cage alone.

Lucas sighed like he had been expecting Luna to protest, "Night is coming," He reminded her, "It is best if it is just him and the Knights in there, they can contain him if…" Lucas looked away quickly.

"If it didn't work." Luna realized that they still weren't sure if the cure would stick. How could they know? They had only used it once, on a cat. A High Wizard was much different, there was already magic there.

"Dinner is about to be served, come and sit with us." Lucas held out his elbow, waiting for Luna to slip her arm through.

"Formal?" Luna asked, slipping her arm through his, "I'm wearing jeans…" She stared down at her clothes.

"The cloak is probably enough." Lucas decided, "No one will see what you're wearing under it."

"Okay." Luna agreed, pulling her cloak closed. She followed Lucas towards the hall where the scent of food was already wafting out to greet them.

Luna's stomach rumbled, reminding her that she hadn't eaten all day. She was starved.

As the doors were opened for them and they stepped inside, Luna felt that strange sensation, it was time to be Lady Blackwater again. She righted her shoulders and smiled as she walked with Lucas to the head table, ready to take her seat beside the King.

Surprisingly the Queen herself was even at the table, though the crowd that gathered at the smaller tables was less than at Luna's last formal meal. She hoped that it wasn't an indication of how quickly the curse was spreading within the Kingdom walls.

"Lady Blackwater." The King tipped his head, "It is good to see you again." He was beaming from ear to ear, the true High Wizard of Eranox had been saved, and as such this was likely Luna's last meal as the ranking High Wizard.

It was a strange status symbol that she wouldn't be sorry to give up. Being stared at by a room filled with strangers as she ate, being watched as she walked through town, waving and smiling at normal people who were really just the same as her.

Ezzie sat on the other side of Lucas at the head table, she leaned forward, "You were busy today, I didn't get to show you around..." She raised a brow.

"Oh, I'm sorry Ezzie," Luna remembered that she had promised her another day on the town, "Can we go out tomorrow?" She asked, "I just wanted to see my father..." It was a sad excuse, she should have said something to Ezzie, instead she had probably left her waiting all day.

Ezzie smirked, "I know, Lucas told me it was important." She rolled her eyes at her brother, "Tomorrow afternoon then, you can spend the morning with your father and we can still explore after." Ezzie suggested with a smile.

"You still haven't even ridden an alicorn." Ezzie had that mischievous look on her face again.

"You're not allowed to ride the alicorn." Lucas hissed, glancing over his sister shoulder like she could have been heard.

"Oh come on Lucas, you know I'm joking." Ezzie giggled, "But I do have to take you to the fountains, out on row Two, you can't leave Eranox without seeing the fountains." Ezzie smiled.

Luna smiled, "That sounds wonderful." She agreed.

"You don't have to..." Lucas muttered under his breath.

"I had a great time with your sister." Luna tilted her head, surprised that Lucas was being so strange, he didn't seem to like Luna hanging out with Ezzie, "I learned a lot from her."

Lucas turned, "Really?" He sounded genuinely surprised, "I didn't think you two would get along…" He trailed off, clearly confused.

"Why not?" Luna asked with a laugh.

"You are from two very different places." Lucas sighed, defeated.

The food was brought forth and a silence washed over the great hall, signaling the end of their conversation.

It was clearly a celebration, the foods that were brought out were delicate and festive, rich and flavorful. Luna was sure that they were celebrating the end of the curse, or at least the beginning of the end. There seemed to be much chatter and laughter echoing in the hall.

Luna was starving, and she was playing the part of Lady Blackwater that evening for the last time, so she decided to sample some of the dishes that she hadn't tried before as they were placed in front of her. She was curious about the different foods that Eranox had to offer and wondered if her mom missed any of them.

A skylight overhead had been opened up, Luna hadn't even noticed that it had been there before, it had been covered with a thick drape since her arrival. She watched it as the shadows grew deeper and soon night had fallen completely.

In the pit of her stomach she was nervous, not about her father, but about the thousands of others that had been cursed and would need to be cured. Another night had come for them and once again they were trapped, there was still a lot of work to be done to return Eranox to what it once was and they were only just beginning to make progress.

Luna turned, Lucas was staring at her again with an inquisitive look on his face, "Are you okay?" He asked.

"Yeah." Luna looked down at her plate, realizing that she had barely touched it, she was so distracted. "Do you think, I mean after my dad is okay to get started…" Luna paused, reorganizing her thoughts, "Do you think I could go home, and let my mom know that I'm okay?" She asked quietly, she had been feeling guilty about it all day.

While she had been busy talking to her dad about her life on Earth and how her mom was doing she had realized that she had been gone longer than she had expected, longer than she had promised. Her mom was probably worried sick, she probably thought the worst had happened to Luna. And the only way to let her know that she was okay was to go home, phones didn't seem to work across portals.

Luna just wanted to see her, and let her know that it was all okay. And maybe if she was lucky, her mom would want to come back with her and start her life over in Eranox with her husband, they could be a *real* family for once.

Lucas nodded, his concern washing away, "Yeah, we should probably get you back and give your mom an update." He agreed again, "I can arrange it for the day after tomorrow, would that be soon enough?" He asked, he sounded nervous about keeping Luna's mom waiting.

"Yeah." Luna nodded, "I wanted to talk to my dad some more in the morning, and spend the afternoon with Ezzie. Then we can maybe plan to leave after that to get her."

"Get her?" Lucas looked confused.

"Yeah, get her." Luna nodded, "If the curse is lifted, I'm sure she'll want to come back, she is from here…" She stared at Lucas, "She would want to come back, right?"

"Maybe" He agreed, but he sounded more like he didn't want Luna to get her hopes up, "I'm sure that there will be loose ends over there that she'll need to tie up, she can't just disappear like you did." He added, "But we *do* need to let her know that you are safe… I *did* promise her that we would keep you safe." He reminded her.

Luna laughed, "Lucas, are you afraid my mom is going to be mad at you?"

Lucas nodded, "Absolutely." His eyes were wide, he wasn't lying.

The doors to the hall slammed open, Luna turned, watching as a Knight stumbled inside, covered in blood. He turned to face the head table, uttering the two words that made Luna's heart stop.

"He escaped."

The Knight collapsed, his blood pooling around him, it was too late for him.

It was like she was frozen, Luna stared at the Knight, the words repeating in her head. It couldn't be possible, she had cured him.

Around her the room began to fill with screams and scraping chairs as chaos erupted from every corner. There was a rush to get out the doors, to get away from the castle.

But Luna just sat there.

She felt Lucas' hand on her arm, tugging her away from the table. But she couldn't move, she just sat and watched, wondering what was happening.

"Luna!" Ezzie's voice cut through the commotion, ringing in Luna's ear.

She turned, seeing the panicked look on Ezzie's face.

It changed everything.

"Ezzie." Luna breathed, snapping out of her daze. They were in danger, and Ezzie looked terrified.

Luna leapt from her seat, reaching past Lucas for Ezzie's arm. She spun around, "Where is the King?" She asked.

Two guards were escorting him and the Queen out of the room. The door closing behind them.

"Come on." Lucas pulled Luna forward, racing for the door.

He reached for the handle but it wouldn't budge. "It's locked." His face turned white. His eyes wide.

Luna could hear the Queen screaming on the other side, wanting her children to be safe. But the door didn't open, they had already locked it on the other side to keep the King and Queen safe from the attack.

"They left us?" Ezzie whispered quietly, her eyes welling with tears.

"Come on Ezzie. We've got you." Luna shook her, snapping her out of her sadness. There would be time for that later.

First they had to get somewhere safe.

EIGHTEEN

The screams were getting louder, coming from inside the dining hall and out in the hallway beyond. Luna tugged Ezzie back towards the head table and ducked beneath it.

It was too late to run, Luna could *feel* it, he was coming.

"Luna, we have to get out of here." Lucas begged, ducking in beside her to try and convince her to leave with him.

"What's happening?" Ezzie quivered, her eyes spilling over with tears.

"It's too late." Luna hissed at Lucas, squeezing Ezzie's hand in her to try to calm her, "He's coming." She whispered, shushing Lucas as she lifted the linen table cloth to peer out into the hall.

"He's here…" Lucas hissed, watching through the small gap as he tucked himself in beside Luna and Ezzie, realizing that hiding had become the better option.

"Who's here?" Ezzie whispered, trying to get a look.

Luna tried to stop her, but it was too late.

Ezzie lifted the tablecloth and stared out into the room, gasping as the dark shape entered the dining hall, tossing a body aside as he walked.

He turned, his eyes falling on Luna.

Ezzie dropped the tablecloth like it was enough to stop him.

"We have to run." Luna screamed, diving out from under the table, her arm pulling at Ezzie behind her.

"Why are we running?" Ezzie asked, following behind Luna as she glanced back at her brother.

"Just do it." Lucas hissed, following up behind.

Luna knew that Lucas could hold his own against the creatures from the Gateway, she had seen him do it before, but Ezzie was another story; she wasn't ready to face a beast like that, Luna had to protect her.

There was only one way out of the room and they had to pass the cursed one to get through. Luna tried to race along the edge of the room, keeping him in her sights as she dashed towards the door, hopeful that he would find another target and allow them to escape without trouble.

She was wrong.

As they neared the door, so close to escaping, the dark creature lunged at her. She dove to the side, keeping Ezzie out of harm's way as she raised her hand towards him.

A ball of fire swept from her palm, but it didn't seem to do anything. Luna was sure that it was just a trick of her eyes, but it almost looked as though he had absorbed it.

She fired again, this time watching more carefully, the fire shone brightly for a moment, and then it disappeared into the dark void that was still standing in front of her.

Magic wouldn't work against him, she should have known, it hadn't really worked against the creatures in the Gateway either. Sure, it had slowed them down a bit, but he was different, he wasn't a commoner, he was a High Wizard who had been turned. There was already more magic coursing through him than Luna could ever hope to know, even cursed, he seemed impervious.

Luna wondered if he had control over it, if he knew what he was doing, if he could stop himself before anyone else got hurt.

She held her arm out towards him, pushing Ezzie behind her, giving her the chance to escape as she faced off against the thing that had been her father earlier that same day.

Luna closed her eyes, trying to feel the curse, searching beneath it for the human that was trapped inside, *you have to stop this*, she pleaded, hoping that he could hear her.

Twisting her hand, Luna tried to feel for the curse, wondering if she could lift it from him without the potion to help her. It seemed an impossible task, the darkness seemed fused to him, unwavering in her mind.

It didn't seem to be working, she could hear him laughing as he moved away from her into the room to find his next victim.

Luna opened her eyes, watching as the dark shape turned away from her, he had already gone farther into the room, he seemed hell-bent on causing chaos. But he had left the door clear for her to escape, so there must have been a small part of her father still in there.

Luna turned around, "We need to get out of her and find somewhere safe." She started towards the door, stopping when she realized that Ezzie was gone.

"Ezzie?" Luna turned, searching through the crowd that was still pressing towards the doors behind her, "Ezzie, where are you?" Luna screamed, worried that she had taken off, or worse, turned back into the dining hall to hide when Luna had closed her eyes.

She had to be there somewhere, she had to be safe.

Luna spun around, searching through the crowd, the screams echoed around her from every side. It was impossible to know where Ezzie would have gone to hide, Lucas didn't seem to be anywhere either.

The room was in chaos, people were running and if they were not they were hiding or injured. The dark man seemed to be reaching for anyone in his path as he stormed the room. Luna could only watch as he threw something at a tall window on the far wall, shattering the glass. A moment later he had leapt through to the other side, ready to maul the rest of the city.

He had been let loose on Eranox, and he seemed determined to spread the curse as far as possible.

Bodies littered the floor.

Very few were dead, but they had all been infected. And now that he was loose in the city, there was no telling who would be left un-cursed at dawn.

Eranox couldn't be saved.

"Where is she?" Lucas shouted, pushing through the crowd to reach Luna, "Where is she?" He asked again, staring wildly at the sea of bodies, searching for his sister.

"I don't know." Luna answered, she was still searching for Ezzie in the crowd escaping through the door, "I closed my eyes, and she was gone." Luna admitted.

She should have kept Ezzie closer, she shouldn't have let her go off on her own, she was supposed to keep her safe.

"We have to find her before he comes back." Lucas turned to the doors, Knights were pushing their way into the room, dressed in their heaviest gear, swords drawn. But they were too late, the Wizard had already escaped.

"He went out the window." Lucas called to them, pointing across the room at the pane of shattered glass. Any number of creatures would be able to get into the castle now, the hall wasn't safe. They had to find somewhere else to go, somewhere safe.

But they had to find Ezzie first.

The Knights rushed towards the window, not wasting any time as they clamored through, ready to take on the creature that had escaped into the night. Luna only hoped that they were prepared, their swords wouldn't do much against him, he was too strong. Lucas had managed to sedate him in the Gateway, but he wouldn't be easily distracted again.

A second wave of Knights entered the room, looking more somber. One by one, they began to round up the bitten, shackling their arms in a row as they scoured the room for victims of the curse.

"What's happening?" Luna asked, still trying to look for Ezzie in the chaos, hoping that she would find her hiding under a table nearby.

"They can't stay… they have been infected." Lucas answered simply, watching the line as it grew longer.

Luna stared with him, most of the bitten were presenting themselves willingly, ready to face the Gateway to save their families from the curse.

It was heart-wrenching to watch, innocent victims dooming themselves to a cursed life in the Gateway until they could be saved. In the pit of her stomach Luna felt sick knowing the truth; the curse couldn't be broken.

Luna looked away, she couldn't watch any longer. Instead she focused her efforts into finding Ezzie, it made it easier to push down the rest of her thoughts if she kept her mind busy.

She couldn't have gotten far, Luna had only been distracted for a moment. There was a good chance that Ezzie had gotten out, found a safe room somewhere in the castle and was waiting for them there. But Luna couldn't leave the hall until she was sure that Ezzie hadn't been left behind.

The truth was, Luna had failed, and in doing so, she had ruined Eranox. There was no cure, and the curse was spreading again, faster than she could have imagined. As she searched through the hall for Ezzie she realized that at least half of the people were lining up to be taken away.

There wouldn't be many un-cursed left in Eranox when the morning came, and even less after the next night. It was Luna's fault, she had believed that she had cured the High Wizard, she had spoken to him all day thinking that he was back to normal. There had been no signs that the curse still lingered in him, she hadn't even thought to check; nothing could have prepared her for what was happening because of her slip up.

Luna pulled back another tablecloth, coming up empty handed again, "I hope she found somewhere safe." Luna turned to Lucas, she was starting to think that Ezzie had gone somewhere else, she hadn't come out to find them yet.

"Prince Lucas, Lady Blackwater..." A Knight appeared behind them, his voice cracking.

Luna turned, her face falling when she saw what the Knight was carrying in his arms.

"Ezzie..." Luna breathed, reaching out to her. The Knight stepped back before Luna could touch her.

"It is too late Lady Blackwater..." He shook his head sadly. "She is one of them now..." He tipped his head towards the sullen crowd waiting to be escorted to their doom by the dining hall doors.

"No..." Lucas stared at the limp form in the Knight's hands, shaking his head in disbelief, "No.. is she..."

"She is alive." The Knight answered, "But that will not make it any easier on her out there." He added sullenly. "I am sorry Prince Lucas, she is going to have to go to the Gateway, I just thought you would want to know... so you can tell the King..." He looked down, avoiding Lucas' stare.

"You can't send her to the Gateway." Lucas decided, his face bitter with anger. "Cage her, lock her up, but she stays here at the castle... she stays *here*." He stared at the Knight, daring him to defy his Prince.

"Lady Blackwater?" The Knight turned to Luna, unsure if he should take the Prince's orders, he had clearly been told to take *all* of the cursed from the incident to the Gateway.

"Do as he requested." Luna used her most noble voice, though the words quivered as they escaped her lips.

"As you wish." The Knight tipped his head, turning to carry Ezzie from the room to another place where she could be kept safe.

Lucas stared after him, his face unreadable, but Luna knew there was rage boiling under the surface.

"Lucas?" Luna placed her hand on his shoulder, "We have to find another way… we can't let this happen to them."

NINETEEN

Lucas and Luna stared out the hall as the line of victims began to depart, led by an entourage of Knights as they prepared to take their walk through the glowing city of Eranox one last time.

"How did this happen." Luna's voice caught in her throat and she realized that she was holding back tears.

Beside her Lucas looked defeated. "We have to tell my father what happened…" He whispered, his voice hollow.

"Should I come with you?" Luna asked, she wasn't sure if Lucas would want to talk to his parents alone, she also wasn't sure what she would do if he did. She had nowhere to go.

"Yeah." Lucas nodded, he wasn't looking forward to telling the King that his daughter had been bitten, that Ezzie had become one of the cursed.

Lucas led Luna out of the dining hall with his head down.

The screams had begun to fade, or perhaps they were just farther away. Knights were scouring the hallway, inspecting each person who had escaped the dining hall in an attempt to weed out those who had been infected.

Every head turned as Luna and Lucas passed, Luna had to stare at her feet to avoid their stares. She was sure that they knew that it was her fault, that they were suffering because she had failed as a High Wizard.

It just felt wrong.

It was the end of Eranox, the fall of the Kingdom; Luna felt the weight on her shoulders as they reached the council room doors.

She wished that she had never come back, Eranox still would have collapsed, but being there to witness it; it was harder than she could have imagined.

There were no less than six Knights standing guard at the doors, "Are you safe?" One of them asked, stepping forward to give them a once over.

Lucas nodded and held out his arms, Luna followed suit. The Knight looked them over, seemingly satisfied that they had not been bitten in the chaos. He nodded his head back at the others and the doors were opened for them.

Inside the King was waiting for them, Madam Hawthorn sat at the table, her eyes rimmed red with tears, she didn't even look up as they entered. Beside her the Queen sat in silence, staring across the room with a forlorn look on her tired face.

"You made it." The King beamed, and then his face fell as the doors closed behind them, "Where is your sister?" He stared, expecting that there was someone behind them, "Where is Ezzie?" He stared at the door, his eyes wide.

Luna took a breath, fearing the answer as she prepared herself to reply, knowing that Lucas wouldn't.

"Bitten." She said slowly.

Across the room the Queen gasped, pulling her hands to her face.

Luna felt her heart flutter with grief.

"I'm so sorry…" She whispered, averting her eyes so she wouldn't see their faces. She couldn't take the looks, the grief that filled the room was enough to drown her already, she couldn't take any more.

"This is the end…" The King walked to the table, taking a seat next to his wife, "Eranox is doomed…" He whispered, hanging his head in defeat.

"It's time to evacuate." Lucas spoke with authority, something that Luna had never heard from him.

The King looked up at him and nodded once.

"It is time." He agreed.

"How can we leave her behind?" The Queen sobbed.

The King reached for her hand, "We have to…" He sighed, "For now…"

"Where are you going to go?" Luna asked, she imagined that they already had a plan, it sounded like Lucas and his father had discussed evacuation before.

"To Earth." Lucas answered flatly.

"To Earth?" Luna stared at him, "All of these people? Where will they go?" Luna asked.

The people of Eranox wouldn't exactly fit in on Earth, especially in River Falls. There were still hundreds of people in Eranox, though come morning there would be fewer, it was still a lot of people to come walking out of the woods in a small town like River Falls.

Someone was bound to notice.

"Renaissance Festival." Lucas answered her question without missing a beat, he had clearly put some thought into it.

"What does that mean?" Luna didn't understand how that would help.

"We are going to convince River Falls that a Renaissance Festival is coming to town." Lucas explained, "Flyers, posters, everything…" He continued, "and then we will make a camp for them there and evacuate Eranox."

It was brilliant, they had clearly been planning their escape for a long time. Luna nodded, surprised at the simplicity of it, "Okay, that will work…"

"We need you two to go and clear the way for us." The King stood, keeping his hand on his wife's shoulder for comfort. "There is a lot of work to be done, both here and on

Earth, you know the plan Lucas, see it through." The King nodded.

"We need to leave tonight." Lucas turned to Luna, the urgency in his voice masking his pain.

"Take three of the Knights with you for the journey." The King sounded scared, and suddenly Luna understood how dangerous their task was.

The Gateway was about to be filled, all of the victims from that night were being marched to the doors as they spoke. If Lucas and Luna survived the trip back to Earth it would be a miracle.

"Understood." Lucas nodded, he crossed the room towards his parents, pulling them both in for a long hug.

Luna looked away, she wanted to let him have his moment, the reality was he might never see them again.

When they finally left the council chambers the halls in the castle had grown quiet. The chaos in the great hall had died down, and the cursed had already been escorted out to the Gateway to suffer their fate.

Lucas didn't say a word as they left the room, and Luna didn't expect that he would be saying anything anytime soon.

"Three of you are coming with us." Luna turned to address the Knights that were waiting in the hallway.

They nodded and separated, prepared to depart with Luna and Lucas back into the Gateway without asking any questions.

Luna walked to her room with the Knights and Lucas in tow. If she was never coming back to Eranox she didn't want to leave anything behind.

She opened her bedroom door and heard a startled gasp from the other side.

"You're alive!" Margie rushed towards her, pulling her in for a hug. A moment later she released Luna, looking embarrassed, "I'm sorry, I know that wasn't proper…" She whispered, averting her eyes.

"I'm glad to see you too." Luna smiled, relieved that the cursed one hadn't found Margie, the only real person in the castle that Luna could talk to.

"Are they evacuating then?" Margie asked in a whisper, following Luna to her wardrobe with a suspicious glance over her shoulder at the Knights standing guard at the door.

"Soon," Luna nodded, "you should tell the others to get ready." Luna paused, "At dawn, when it is safe…" She added, she didn't want Margie to get bitten, she was starting to like having her around.

"I will do, thank you Lady Blackwater." She whispered, still keeping her eyes on the Knights.

Luna filled her school bag, she was already wearing sneakers and her Earth clothes, though the cloak over her shoulders wasn't from Earth, she decided to keep it on. It was warm, and would remind her of her adventures in Eranox when it was all over and she had to move on with her life.

With one last look around the room, she pulled Margie in for a hug and said goodbye.

It was time to leave Eranox behind for good.

TWENTY

Luna followed the Knights in silence as they walked to Lucas' room on the other side of the castle to retrieve him. He had gone ahead to gather his things. It seemed that he had already been prepared for the evacuation, he was standing in the door, staring at his room with a bag over his shoulder when they arrived.

    Luna stood back, giving him some space as he said goodbye to his home in Eranox. She was sure that he was having a hard time with it, how could he not, Eranox had been his home, and it was about to be lost forever under an unbreakable curse.

    Lucas turned away from his room slowly, closing the door over, his face still and unreadable.

    "Let's go." Luna nodded to the Knights as they waited for instruction. "We are going through the Gateway, starting the evacuation." She added, feeling that it was fair to give them a warning that they would not be returning.

    The flash of panic in their eyes lasted only a moment and then they began to march down the hall, keeping pace with Lucas and Luna as they walked towards the castle doors.

    The night was passing quickly and Luna was determined to keep moving forward, she would sleep when she was home safe. There were still more obstacles in their way, and she had to keep herself alert and prepared.

They still had to get through the Gateway.

Luna fingered the necklace around her throat to be sure that it was still there. She didn't want to be left behind, not in the maze of creatures, not when it was about to be filled with more of them.

The city was less than quiet as they passed through the castle gates and into the streets. Screams and howls echoed through the spaces between the buildings, creatures watching as they passed. Her father, the cursed one, was still out there within Eranox, he hadn't been caught yet; Luna could feel him out there spreading the curse.

No one watched them through the windows that night as they passed the boarded up storefronts that had gone dark with fear.

Eranox *felt* defeated.

Ahead there was a crowd, the cursed of that night, waiting to enter the Gateway. The infection had not yet taken hold, they stood in silence, scared and shivering as they waited for dawn when they would join the others.

Lucas slowed.

"She's there…" He whispered, staring ahead.

Luna followed his gaze.

There in the middle of the crowd was a girl wearing a beautiful orange dress, her hair was tousled and her eyes brimmed with tears, but it was her.

Ezzie hadn't been kept at the castle.

"Why would they bring her here?" Luna asked, afraid of the answer.

Lucas didn't answer right away, he stared at his sister for a moment longer before he finally looked away, "If we left her alone in the castle, she would die…" He whispered, "She needs to be with them to survive…" He gritted his teeth.

"Should we…"

"No." Lucas answered sharply, "It would only make it harder… for all of us…" He stayed back from the crowd, trying to hide from his sister before she spotted him.

Luna stared past the crowd at the doors to the Gateway, they only opened during the day, for the safety of the inhabitants. However a ladder had been erected against the wall, the same as the night they had come for Alec Blackwater.

"I think they intend for us to hurry." A Knight turned, tipping his head to Luna.

"I think so." Luna frowned, she wasn't quite prepared to venture back into the night maze, but it seemed that the King intended them to finish the trip in one night. Which meant that they would have to travel quickly and hope that they didn't encounter any danger.

"Eranox will be waiting at the gate tomorrow at dusk." Lucas whispered, staring at the ladder as though he had been expecting it.

"So soon?" Luna asked, "Will we have time to prepare for them?"

"They need to evacuate." Lucas replied, starting to walk towards the ladder, "We will have to make it work."

The Knights followed them past the crowd, venturing up the ladder ahead of the two of them to secure the other side.

Soon, Lucas and Luna were making their way back up over the wall and into the Gateway, leaving Eranox behind one final time.

A fourth Knight followed behind them and as they landed safely on the other side he began to hoist the rope ladder back up, leaving them in the Gateway with nowhere to go but Earth.

"Lead the way." Luna turned to Lucas, ready to get home and put the nightmare behind her.

"This way." Lucas started forward at a jog.

The night was already almost half over, if they hoped to get through the portal before dawn they were going to have to hurry.

Luna stared at the tall stone walls as she jogged behind Lucas, knowing that she would never have to see them again.

For her it was the end of an adventure, a horrible one, but still an adventure. It was her final trek through the maze that she would never see again, there was something strange about the experience, she found herself knowing that she would miss it.

And then came the guilt. While Luna was reminiscing about her wild adventure, she knew that Lucas and the Knights were having a much different experience as they raced through the Gateway. They were leaving their home, saying goodbye to everything they had ever known, not even knowing if their loved ones and friends were going to make it through to join them in the new world on the other side.

Though Lucas had been to Earth, Luna watched as the Knights stared ahead with apprehension, Earth was going to be stranger than they feared. Even with the caravan and the ruse of a Renaissance Fair, there were too many things that would be different for them.

Like electricity.

Lucas wound them through the Gateway faster, cautious of the noises that echoed through the tall walls. It seemed that the creatures were waiting for the newly cursed to join them, the farther they got from Eranox, the quieter the Gateway became.

Luna was running out of breath, but the moons overhead were getting low in the sky and they needed to get to the portal before it closed.

"Only a little farther." Lucas huffed, hurrying to make it around another turn.

The Knights seemed to be having a more difficult time keeping up, their heavy armor jangled against them as they tried to keep pace, they were more protected against an attack, but the weight of the metal plates must have been exhausting to carry all that way.

Lucas dove around another bend and Luna could hear him slowing down before she made the turn.

They had made it.

The fireflies swirled around the door, greeting them with a frenzy of excited flickers.

It was time to go home.

TWENTY ONE

When the fireflies finally appeared, Luna was the only one who seemed excited to see them.

"I'll let you say goodbye," Luna smiled, "see you on the other side." She tipped her head to Lucas and the Knights before she turned back to the door, pressing her hand against the wood and allowing herself to be carried through to Earth; leaving Lucas and the Knights a chance to say their final goodbyes in private.

The air rushed through her hair and a moment later her feet found the ground. She took a deep breath and stepped away from the grove before she could be taken back through.

There was a cool chill in the night, Luna pulled her cloaks tightly around her, glad that she had chosen to keep them with her to remember Eranox, because in that moment she was cold, and it bit right to the bones.

Autumn had turned cold on Earth, and Eranox had remained the same balmy temperature. Her return to Earth's weather had certainly come as a shock, she hoped that the others would be prepared for it when they evacuated. Nights on Earth were much colder than those in the other world.

Soon there was another flash. Lucas and the Knights appeared in the clearing.

Lucas looked the same, but the Knights eyes were wide with surprise.

"This is it?" One of them whispered to the others, looking around the clearing with curiosity.

"This way." Luna called to them, she lead the way down the path away from the portal to her home.

It felt good to be back on Earth with the dangers behind them, though the heavy weight of the fate of Eranox still hung in the air, it seemed farther away for a moment.

"The light is on." Luna turned to Lucas, that meant her mom was waiting for them.

Luna hurried out of the woods and across the backyard towards the back door of the house, suddenly nervous. What was her mom going to think of the escort that had arrived with her, surely she would presume the worst; and she wouldn't be wrong.

The back door slid open and her mom came rushing out before she had even made it to the back patio.

"Luna!" Her mom ran towards her, pulling her in for a hug, "I'm so glad you are okay." She held Luna tightly, "Thank you for bringing her back Lucas." She smiled.

Lucas shuffled his feet uncomfortably, seemingly a bit relieved that he had managed to keep his promise.

"Let's have a look at you." Luna's mom held her arms out, stepping back to look her daughter over. "I *love* your robes." She leaned back to take a better look at the new cloak that Luna wore over her shoulders, "You look like a real High Wizard…" Her eyes twinkled.

And then she saw the Knights.

Her face fell in an instant, "What happened?" She whispered, leading Luna and Lucas back into the house, "Why are they here?" She glanced back at the three Knights waiting in the backyard.

The Knights waited out back, clearly unsure if they were meant to keep guard.

"Come in." Luna called back to them, "There is no danger here."

The Knights clunked into the house through the back door, suddenly their armor seemed quite out of place as they tried to squeeze in around the couch to find room to stand.

Luna's mom walked towards the kitchen and put on the kettle, rummaging through the cupboards for snacks, "Get in here and tell me what happened." She called over her shoulder to Lucas and Luna, "Did it work?" She asked, carrying an armful towards the table.

Luna paused for a moment, staring at her mom. Luna could tell by her eagerness that she thought Luna had returned to tell her it was working, breaking the news was going to break her heart.

"Why don't we sit for this…" Lucas suggested, holding a chair out for Luna's mom.

"That doesn't sound good…" She slid in to the seat at the table growing quiet, her glances towards the Knights becoming more suspicious.

"Do you want to tell her." Lucas asked Luna as he sat at the table, his voice cracked and Luna knew that she was going to have to do it. He was still reeling from the loss of his sister.

Luna nodded and found herself a chair.

"It can't be that bad…" Luna's mom was staring at her, her face was quiet and unreadable, she was preparing herself for the news.

"It did work…" Luna sighed, "at first…"

"It did?" The eagerness returned and Luna had to continue before her mom hopped up to get more cookies for the table.

Luna reached for her mom's hand, holding her still so she could explain.

"They asked me to test the cure on a cat first." She explained, "And it worked, the curse lifted from it easily." She continued slowly, "So they decided that we should try him next,

Alec Blackwater, so they could have another High Wizard to help, so we could cure them faster…"

"You saw him?" Luna's mom gasped.

"I did." Luna nodded, remembering her talk with Alec, and how she had wanted to visit him again and would never get the chance to. She cleared her throat, "He was cured," Luna smiled sadly, "for a while day, I even got to talk to him…" She felt a lump rising in her throat again, "And then night came… and it didn't work…"

"Oh, Luna." Her mom squeezed her hand, "That must have been so hard…"

Luna nodded, trying to compose herself.

"But they can probably find a way to make it stick, right?" She glanced at Lucas, "They just need more time?" She looked back at Luna, "You need to go back there?"

Luna shook her head, "He escaped, in the castle…" Luna stared, her mom's face falling from sadness to horror, "He spread the curse, he… he attacked everyone." Luna bit her lip, "Eranox is evacuating… it's over." She looked down at the table, she didn't want to see the look on her mom's face, not then, not after she just told her that her home world was ruined.

The room was silent for a long time, the hiss of the kettle on the stove sounded far away, even the Knights had stopped moving, the clink of their rustling armor growing silent as they waited for something to happen.

"Lucas?" Luna's mom broke the silence, staring across the table, her eyes soft, "What can I do to help?"

Luna looked up, her mom seemed less distraught than she had expected, she was sure that she was imagining it, but there still seemed to be a hint of hope in her eyes.

"We need a place for them all." Lucas began, "The council has taken my advice, they will be arriving under the guise of a traveling Renaissance Festival. We will need flyers up around town, and some tents for them and supplies." Lucas wrung his hands together, "They should be okay out there." He looked at the woods through the back door.

"That sounds very clever…" Luna's mom smiled, "When do they arrive?"

"They will be traveling the Gateway during the day, they should arrive at nightfall." Lucas answered urgently.

"Okay, then we will have some work to do." She nodded, rising from the table without another word.

A moment later she walked past Luna with a tray of treats and tea, presenting it to the Knights in the living room with a strange curtsy as she spoke to them in a hushed tone.

"She took that well." Luna stared at her mom, curious.

"A little too well." Lucas agreed, "Do you think she knew that it would fail?" He asked, "She really didn't want you going with me, maybe she knew…" He sighed.

"No," Luna shook her head, turning back to Lucas, "This is something else…"

Luna stared out at her mom, she was still talking to the Knights, her voice barely above a whisper. They seemed to be smiling.

Her mom glanced back and caught Luna staring. She excused herself and walked back towards the kitchen, the twinkle still in her eye.

"Come with me." She hissed as she entered the kitchen, reaching for Luna's arm, "You too." She turned to Lucas.

Her eyes were bright with excitement.

TWENTY TWO

Luna followed her mom through the kitchen to her office with Lucas behind her.

"What's going on?" Lucas whispered, watching as Luna's mom closed and locked the office door behind them.

"When you left Luna, I had some thinking to do…" She turned to her laptop waiting for it to warm up, "I was so proud of you for not giving up, really I was ashamed that I had."

"Really?" Luna stepped towards her, "So you found the mirror?" She asked, her excitement building.

Her mom shook her head, "No. I don't think I ever will, it's guarded too well." She sighed, "But I might have found something else." She started typing on her computer.

"Something that will help Eranox?" Lucas asked, leaning forward, his voice eager.

"Maybe." Luna's mom stopped typing, and turned the computer to face them.

The Saneville Sleuths read the title of the web page that her mom had opened.

"A blog?" Luna didn't get it.

"Not just any blog…" Luna's mom scrolled down, "No one knows this much about Hobgoblins and Gnomes without seeing them for real…"

Lucas looked at her like she had a second head, "You think this person, the person who wrote these… knows how to get to Avidaura?" He asked.

"I think they've *been* to Avidaura." Luna's mom answered.

"So they could help us, they might know where the mirror is, or another way through…" Luna felt her chest lightening, "We can still get help.…"

"Eranox can still be saved." Lucas smiled.

"It's a long shot." Luna's mom had turned serious, "And it's going to take time, but I think it might work. It's at least worth checking out." She added.

"What about the evacuation?" Luna turned to Lucas, the King and what was left of Eranox would be arriving in a day, and they still had to prepare.

"We will still have to prepare for the evacuation," Lucas nodded, "they can't stay there…"

"Yes." Luna's mom agreed, "They will still have to come through, we can keep them safe while we look into this."

"And when my father arrives, we can tell him. I am sure that he will agree, it is worth looking into…" Lucas was beaming, though Luna knew that they were still a long way away from saving Eranox.

"So it's settled then." Luna's mom clapped her hands together, "We aren't giving up, not yet."

Lucas nodded, his smile was contagious.

"How long have you two been up?" Luna's mom changed the subject suddenly, "Dawn is coming soon, and I imagine you have been traveling for some time…" She raised her eyebrow, giving Luna a once over.

"A long time." Lucas answered, "But there is a lot that needs to be done, I already had the posters made…" He shook his head, "They are at my house, over on the back lane, the one that has a for sale sign."

"So it's been *you* squatting there." Luna's mom laughed, "Good to know." She smiled. "Why don't you two get a bit of sleep, I can get started on the posters before the town wakes up…"

"Oh, I almost forgot," She stopped, shaking her head, "That friend of yours stopped by, Jess, I told her you were out of town visiting family for a week."

"Thanks mom." Luna yawned, realizing how tired she was.

"Lucas, you can take my room." She tipped her head towards the stairs as she opened the office door.

***

Luna woke up at noon, surprisingly fully rested after her long adventure. Though she was tempted to roll over and try to sleep a little longer, she knew that the rest of Eranox was arriving at nightfall, and there was a lot that probably still needed to be done before their arrival.

Lucas was already downstairs, though Luna's mom was nowhere to be found.

"She went to pick up more tents and tarps." Lucas answered her question before she could even ask it.

"And the Knights?" Luna looked around, surprised that she couldn't hear them.

"In the woods, getting everything ready." Lucas, opened the fridge, emptying the bag in his arms.

"You need a hand?" Luna asked, not sure what else there was to do.

"Yeah, there is a load of groceries on the front steps, it all needs sorted."

"Got it." Luna walked towards the front door and opened it, there were more bags of food than she had ever seen in her life.

Luna wasn't sure how they were going to afford keeping up with all of the new visitors, but she was sure that her mom would find a way. She carried as many as she could manage back into the kitchen where Lucas was rummaging through another pile.

"Cold stuff in the fridge, if you can find room, everything else goes out back to the Knights."

Luna looked down at the bags in her arms, there didn't seem to be anything that needed to be kept cold, "I'll take this out back then."

She walked to the back doors, they were already open, saving her having to put the bags down. She could see the Knights before she had even stepped out the door, they were busy tying tarps and fabric across from tree to tree. The place was really shaping up nicely, though it would never be anything compared to the *real* Eranox.

She walked towards them, staring out into the trees, they had cut back the brush, making room for living in the forest with ease.

As she approached one of the Knights stopped, walking to greet her. He had taken off his helmet and most of his metal plates to make it easier to work. He smiled at Luna, a twinkle in his eye.

"I can take those." He tipped his head at the groceries in Luna's arms, "Here." He held out his arms so Luna could pile them up.

"It looks really nice out here." She smiled, "Is there anything I can help with?"

He considered for a moment, turning to look at the other Knights working behind him, "I'm not sure there is much that you could do out here, no magic, all has to be done by hand…." He shook his head.

"I guess that will take some getting used to." Luna chuckled, "I'll go get some more food for you." She turned back to the house.

By mid-afternoon when her mom finally returned, the forest was ready for Eranox to arrive.

It looked like a festival, event tents and tarps as far as the eye could see. Luna imagined that the residents of River Falls would believe the ruse for a while, they would probably even come to visit them, thinking that they were a real Renaissance Festival.

Luna just hoped that the Eranoxians, after a tiresome evacuation, were up to entertaining the strangers that would come to see them in the new world. It was going to be a lot for them to get used to.

Lucas and Luna were sitting at the table, counting down the hours until the portal could be opened.

"Are you just going to sit there until night falls?" Luna's mom asked, walking into the kitchen to start the kettle again.

"Yes." Lucas answered anxiously.

"How do we get that many people through?" Luna asked, she knew that she wasn't able to pass through the portal without her necklace, did everyone in Eranox carry a piece of the stone with them?

"A human chain with enough stones should get them through." Lucas answered, "But you and I have to go down and hold it open." He added.

"Hold it open?" Luna frowned, "How does that work, can't you just go through?"

"I already explained it to the Knights." Lucas leaned forward, "They'll have to tether us here, and then we go through, we get stuck halfway. Eranox comes through, and then they pull us back."

"Is that safe?" Luna's mom asked, she had been listening from the kitchen.

"I've done it once before." Lucas answered, "It should be just as safe as going through normal." He assured her.

"How long until nightfall?" Luna asked, glancing out the window, the Knights were still unloading her mom's car from the last trip, carrying it all out into the woods.

"Hours." Lucas sighed, leaning back in his chair and staring at the ceiling.

"How many do you think are left?" Luna asked quietly.

"Left?" Her mom slid in at the table with a pot of tea and an armful of mugs, "How bad was it?"

"It was pretty bad." Luna answered, still waiting for Lucas to answer her question.

"There were so many at the gates last night…" Lucas stared off, "I have no idea how many will be left…"

Luna's mom filled the silence, pouring them tea.

"Let's go check on the camp." She suggested, nodding her head towards Luna.

Luna got up and followed her, leaving Lucas alone at the table, still staring at nothing.

"Is he okay?" Luna's mom asked when they were finally outside and out of earshot.

"He's nervous, I'm sure of it. His family is out there right now, waiting in the Gateway for night to fall…" Luna sighed, "and with all of the people that got cursed last night… even Ezzie, oh…" Luna glanced back.

"Ezzie?" Her mom prodded.

"His sister." Luna answered, "She was bitten, and they sent them all, all the ones that were cursed, into the Gateway. She's out there right now, while the rest of Eranox is waiting to be saved…"

"The wait must be driving him crazy…" Luna's mom observed, "He doesn't know if the rest of his family is okay?"

"We can't make time go any faster." Luna sighed as they reached the tree line and entered the camp.

"It is all ready." One of the Knights called to them, he had taken a seat at the base of a tree and was resting his eyes, he didn't even look up to see who was walking towards him.

"Looks good down here." Luna's mom walked around, looking at the tarps and tents with a sense of nostalgia that made Luna stare at her.

"Hey Mom…" Luna followed behind her, curious.

"Yeah?" she glanced back.

"Do we have any other family in Eranox?" She asked quietly, afraid that she was about to send her mom through some memories that weren't so pleasant.

It occurred to Luna a moment too late that even if they *did* have other family in Eranox, they could already have been cursed.

"Yes Luna." Her mom answered whimsically, "Your dad was an only child, and his parents had both passed before we left, but I had some family still… I wonder if you met any of them…" She stared at Luna.

"I don't know…" Luna smiled, glad that her mom was finally talking about her life in Eranox, she seemed so much happier despite the evacuation. It was like she was getting to go home, except her home was coming to her.

"Come on, sit down." Luna's mom found herself a seat at a table in the camp, waving Luna towards her, "You need to hear some more about Eranox." She smiled, her eyes twinkling.

Luna was still listening to her mom's stories when Lucas appeared in the camp a few hours later, "Am I interrupting anything?" He slid in at the picnic table and waited for a reply.

"Oh, Lucas, I was just telling Luna about… well… life before the curse…" She shook her head, "It must be close to nightfall." She looked up at the dimming sky.

"Are the tethers ready?" Lucas asked, searching for a Knight who might have an answer.

"We should get ready." Luna agreed, rising from the small table to stretch her legs, "It won't be long."

Lucas nodded and disappeared into the camp to find one of the Knights who could help him.

"Are you ready for it?" Luna's mom asked.

"Yeah, Lucas said he's done it before, it should be fine." She smiled, leaning in to give her mom a hug, "I'm going to go wait for him in the clearing, I'll see you when it's over."

"Okay, I love you Luna." Her mom smiled.

"I love you too mom." Luna hugged her again and started towards the clearing.

It was hard to find when you weren't taking the path, she found herself lost in the camp trying to find a way out for several minutes before she finally caught a glimpse of a firefly flickering as it prepared for the night.

"There it is." Luna sighed, pushing her way through the tarps to the clearing on the other side.

Lucas was already waiting with a strange harness strapped over his shoulders, behind him one of the Knights was tying the rope to a tree.

"You should get ready." Lucas pointed to a second harness.

Luna felt for the stone around her neck, carefully checking that it was still intact before she started to strap herself in.

"Make sure that the straps are secure Lady Blackwater." The Knight finished his knot on Lucas' rope and moved towards her, "You will be tied off, we will pull you in when they are all through."

"Okay." Luna was a little nervous about hanging in the place between worlds, but Lucas had assured her that it would be fine, though that didn't make her any less worried.

"All set." The Knight called to her a moment later, Luna turned back to check her rope, giving it a tug to make sure that it was secure.

"Come on." Lucas had stepped forward to the place where the portal would appear, he was watching the sky as it grew darker.

"You ready?" Luna asked, stepping forward to his side.

"I just want to get this done with." He admitted, a nervous smile on his face.

Fireflies flickered around them, swirling as they prepared for night to fall and the portal to be activated by the two waiting travelers.

Luna took a deep breath, and then it happened.

There was a flash and she felt herself pulled forward. The harness bit into her shoulders and she screamed. She hadn't been expecting it to be so sudden. She had been pulled into the space between Earth and Eranox, the light was blinding, even with her eyes closed.

She tried to reach up and cover her eyes with her hands, but the force pulling against her was incredible. She wasn't sure how the Knights would be able to pull her out of it, and she certainly couldn't reach her harness.

She could feel the others passing by, like a train passing by while she was standing on the platform, they rushed by her in a surge. And then it stopped.

Suddenly a strange panic set in. She couldn't see where she was, she couldn't move, and she was sure that she was about to be trapped in the portal.

Then she felt the tug.

Luna whipped back, landing hard on the ground, her head spinning. Someone was screaming beside her, she reached for the rope, giving it a tug to see if she had landed on the right side. She still couldn't see, her eyes were burning from the bright light, struggling to readjust to the darkness around her.

For a second she thought that she had gone through to Eranox, and then she reached the end of the rope and felt the tree; she was back home.

The screaming came again, right next to her, it was a guttural sound, pained and raspy. Luna turned, still trying to see the clearing, "What's happening, who's hurt?" She asked, hoping that someone would hear her.

"It's the Queen dear," Margie's hand landed on her shoulder, "she's in labor."

TWENTY THREE

By the time the spots had faded from Luna's eyes enough to see again, the Queen had been carried off. Lucas stood next to her, still rubbing his eyes, his harness still fastened around him.

"Luna?" He turned, blinking until he could see, "Where did they take her?" His eyes were wide, he knew what was happening.

Luna reached for her straps, trying to unfasten herself so she could find out, "I don't know, but the baby is coming." She whispered, though by then the whole camp must have known, the Queen's agonizing screams echoed through the trees.

Luna would be surprised if half of River Falls hadn't noticed.

"Could you help me get out of this?" Lucas was struggling with the straps on his harness, trying to get out so fast that he couldn't get the buckle to release.

"Calm down." Luna stared into his wild eyes, reaching for the clasp and clicking the button, "She's going to be fine…" Luna assured him.

"She just went through a portal," Lucas reminded her, "I don't even know what happens to a baby when it goes through a portal…." He was already walking away, leaving Luna to rush after him.

"My mom came through when she was pregnant with me." Luna shouted, trying to keep up, "And I turned out fine…." She trailed off, not sure that she was the best example, she had messed up the cure and left Eranox in an evacuation, there was no telling how portal jumping really affected a baby.

Lucas followed the sounds of his mother screaming, and Luna followed him. Eranoxians moved quickly out of their way as they rushed through the bustling camp trying to figure out where the Queen had been taken.

Finally then ran into Luna's mom. She was standing outside of a camping tent, her arms crossed over with worry.

"Is she in there?" Lucas asked, taking a step towards the tent as his mother screamed again.

Luna's mom held out her hand, "Not now Lucas, there isn't room for you." She held him back.

"A tent?" Luna stared at her mom.

"I offered them the house, but she was already too far along…" She shook her head, "It was this or the forest…"

"Are they going to be okay?" Lucas asked, his face was pale, he still hadn't stepped back, Luna's mom was holding him up with the arm that she had put out to stop him from moving forward.

"She should be okay, and the baby too." Luna's mom turned Lucas away from the tent to face her, trying to calm him down. "The portal puts a lot of pressure on the body," She tried to explain calmly, "and your mother was very pregnant, that baby was coming any day… the jump just helped her along." She smiled, tipping her head to Luna, "Same happened with that one…" She smiled.

Lucas' mom stopped screaming and another cry came from inside the tent. Lucas turned back, "Is that?…"

"That would be the baby." Luna's mom nodded, "Sounds like everything was okay."

Lucas took a step towards the tent.

"You should give them a moment." Luna's mom cautioned.

"What now?" Luna asked, the camp was bustling around them, the Knights seemed to be getting everyone settled on their own.

"I'm going to head back to the house, get them some clean blankets." Luna's mom turned towards a break in the trees, "Let me know if they need anything else?" She suggested, disappearing into the darkness.

***

The night was long as Eranox moved into the camp, even longer as the Queen's transition onto Earth included the arrival of a new son.

Luna waited with Lucas outside of the tent where Margie had ushered the Queen to give birth. The baby had arrived over an hour ago, and the King had already departed to deal with other duties, but Lucas was still waiting patiently outside to meet his new sibling.

"Are you sure you don't want me to go?" Luna asked him for the fifth time in as many minutes. He seemed nervous about meeting the baby on his own, she was sure that he was just wishing that Ezzie was there with him.

"No, stay, you should meet him, and she might need something…" Lucas nodded, pausing as the flap to the tent finally opened and Margie poked her head out.

"Prince Lucas, Lady Blackwater," She nodded to each, "the Queen would like to see you." She beamed.

Lucas took a deep breath and walked forward, Luna followed behind.

The Queen was sitting in a small cot that had been brought into the camp for her to use. In her arms was a small bundle wrapped in blankets.

"He's so strange looking." Lucas looked down at his new brother.

"You looked the same." His mom answered tiredly.

"I wish Ezzie was here…" Lucas whispered, reaching one finger towards his brother.

"I do too dear." His mom smiled sadly, leaning back as though she was about to fall asleep.

"She's going to need to rest dears." Margie whispered, quickly she shooed Lucas and Luna out of the tent.

Lucas led the way out of the tent and back into the camp. It was hard to think that only a few hours earlier the whole place had been empty, now that Eranox had arrived there were people everywhere.

"You can stay at the house tonight if you want." Luna suggested, "Give your parents some time with the baby…"

Lucas chuckled sadly, "Ezzie was right, the baby got to go to Earth before her."

"There is still a way, she can still be cured." Luna reminded him of her mom's findings.

"And if it turns out to be nothing?" Lucas was starting to sound skeptical.

"Then we find the mirror." She answered, more determined than ever.

"We're still going to have to talk to him, my dad, about that blog." Lucas shook his head, "It's going to be impossible to explain to him… you know because if the internet thing…" He stared ahead at the house.

Luna fell silent as they crossed the backyard to the house. Lucas was right, trying to tell the King that they had found a lead wasn't the hard part, figuring out how to explain the internet, and computers; it wouldn't be easy.

When they walked in the back door they found that the King was sitting with Luna's mother deep in conversation.

"Oh good, you're back." Luna's mom waved Luna and Lucas over.

"Lady Blackwater, Lucas." The King tipped his head in greeting, "How is your new brother doing, has she given him a name yet?" He asked.

"No," Lucas shook his head, "Not yet, I think she was going to get some rest."

"I was telling your father about the information I found, that place that might have some answers." Luna's mom smiled, she had clearly found a way to explain it to the King without confusing him.

"It does sound like we might finally have a way to get to the old Avidauran council, even without finding the Mirror here on Earth." The King tipped his head to Luna's mom, "There might still be a way to get Eranox back..."

"I was hoping you would approve." Lucas watched his father's face, "I would like to go and see..." He sounded like he was asking for permission.

The King shook his head, "Normally I would prefer to send Knights," He looked at Lucas, frowning, "But you are the one who has learned about this world." He waved his hand at the inside of the house, clearly it was strange to him.

"So I can go?" Lucas asked.

"Yes, I think you should be the one to go, and perhaps Lady Blackwater should accompany you." He nodded.

Luna nodded her head, watching her mom for confirmation that it was okay for her to accept. Her mom was smiling.

"I should get back to your mother Lucas, it has been a long and trying night." The King rose from the table, "In the morning we will discuss your departure, for now I should go and be with your mother." He turned towards the door, a Knight already waiting to guide him through the camp.

Luna's mom sighed and slumped forward. "Okay." She looked up, "I need you two to see something, and then I think we all need some sleep."

"What did you find?" Lucas asked, following her back to her office.

"There was a new post today." She turned her laptop around so they could see, "Dark Fairies." She smiled, "And I *know* you can only find them in Avidaura..."

"So you think it's real then?" Lucas skimmed through the blog, glancing over the posts.

"It has to be." Luna stared, "And look at the picture…" Luna leaned in, *"Home of the Saneville Saints…"* She read the banner. "I know how to find them."

Luna's mom closed her computer, standing behind her desk with a wild look in her eyes, "What do you think Luna? Is it time for your first quest?"

Luna smiled, "I'm in."

ABOUT THE AUTHOR

Katlin Murray lives in Ontario with her husband and two boys. When Katlin isn't in her office typing or on film sets, she enjoys going on adventures with her boys in the great outdoors.

Learn more at: Katlinmurray.com
Or
Avidaura.com

Made in the USA
Monee, IL
04 November 2019